The Adventures of the Little Tin Tortoise

A Self-Esteem Story with Activities
for Teachers, Parents and Carers

Deborah Plummer

Illustrations by Jane Serrurier

Jessica Kingsley Publishers
London and Philadelphia

First published in 2006
by Jessica Kingsley Publishers
116 Pentonville Road
London N1 9JB, UK
and
400 Market Street, Suite 400
Philadelphia, PA 19106, USA

www.jkp.com

Library of Congress Cataloging in Publication Data
Plummer, Deborah.
   The adventures of the Little Tin Tortoise : a self-esteem story with activities for teachers, parents, and carers / Deborah Plummer.
      p. cm.
   Includes bibliographical references.
   ISBN-13: 978-1-84310-406-3 (pbk. : alk. paper)
   ISBN-10: 1-84310-406-7 (pbk. : alk. paper) 1. Self-esteem in children. 2. Self-esteem--Study and teaching (Elementary) I. Title.
   BF723.S3P57 2006
   649'.7--dc22

                                                                                        2005022440

British Library Cataloguing in Publication Data
A CIP catalogue record for this book is available from the British Library

ISBN-13: 978 1 84310 406 3
ISBN-10: 1 84310 406 7

Printed and bound in Great Britain by
Athenaeum Press, Gateshead, Tyne and Wear

This book is dedicated to
the memory of Lovena Seevathean
and to her baby daughter Yovena,
who is her precious gift to the world

Acknowledgements

My desire to write this book has its origins in the creativity of my parents, Chris and Berna, who coloured my childhood with their story-telling.

My grateful thanks go to Jane Serrurier, a gifted primary school teacher and consummate story-teller whose talents and determination never cease to inspire me. She was the first person to hear the story of the little tin tortoise and has given a great deal of her time to read through the different stages of this book and to make many helpful suggestions and comments. She has also provided the illustrations that appear throughout.

Dorothy Clarke, a speech and language therapist and Colleen Carpen, a nurse at a children's unit in Cambridge, have been fantastically supportive and have also given generously of their time to reading and commenting on the manuscript.

I am also grateful to Savitri, Coumaren, Lovena and Yo who helped me to fall in love with their beautiful, vibrant country and whose generosity leaves me breathless.

A note on the text

All the characters in this book are fictitious and any resemblance to actual persons is purely coincidental.

Please note that throughout Part 1 of the text the pronouns 'he' and 'she' have been used interchangeably.

Contents

Part 1

Theoretical and Practical Background

1

Introduction

There are, of course, many factors that will influence a child's levels of self-esteem. Environmental and relationship factors in particular are known to play a huge part in the development of feelings of self-worth and competency. Studies in this field also show that both negative and positive interactions can directly affect the long term chemical balance and neurological structure of an infant's developing brain.

The task of helping troubled children to regain self-esteem, or indeed to build self-esteem where none exists, is therefore a complex and multi-layered undertaking. This book, while acknowledging the difficulty of such a task for some children, focuses on the elements of self-esteem that are potentially within each child's ability to manage. As parents, teachers or carers we have a vital role to play in helping young children to explore and develop these important foundation elements (see p.17). One of the ways in which we can do this is through the medium of story.

Throughout childhood (and, in fact, throughout life) the building and maintenance of healthy self-esteem is intimately linked with our 'imaginative' abilities. Story-telling, in all its many forms, provides an important means of fostering this link. Through stories, children have the opportunity to *imagine* life; to begin to understand that what we *think* affects the way that we experience and influence our environment and the events and relationships that we encounter.

The Adventures of the Little Tin Tortoise arose from my own exploration of this link in the context of my clinical practice as a speech and language therapist. For many years I have used story books as part of the therapy process with young children, both during group work and in individual therapy. These stories have proved to be an invaluable tool for helping children to explore issues related to communication needs, difficulties and strengths.

In common with many practitioners, I have also found that introducing an interactive element to stories provides an opening for children to explore their feelings in a safe and respectful way. So for example, I might stop at a relevant point in the story and say 'I wonder what this little boy is feeling right now' or 'Can you guess why she was so angry?' This interaction invariably encourages children to volunteer creative thoughts and sometimes to make up their own stories in a way that reveals a wonderful, innate capacity for using metaphors.

Continued experimentation with this approach eventually led me to write the story of the little tin tortoise. For me, this character represents a vital quality of healthy self-esteem – that of 'joyful resilience'. Inevitably, we will all face difficult situations and strong emotions in life, but children with low self-esteem are often overwhelmed by their feelings and tend to have unrealistic ideas about what they think they 'should' be able to achieve. Many children believe that they are incapable of trying new things or have a heightened fear of failure which prevents them from exploring life's possibilities.

In the story, the tortoise is eventually able to master the joyful ability to move freely without this incapacitating fear. It copes with a few 'trials' and setbacks and, with the help of friends, discovers its identity through determination and through building emotional resilience. The introduction to the story, echoed again in the final line, suggests the possibility that we can all find the courage to make this journey because, although the story is set a long time ago, 'it only happened yesterday and today. Or maybe it will happen tomorrow – and that is its magic!'

For ease of use the book is divided into three parts. Part 1 gives a brief introduction to the 'art' of story-telling and the nature of healthy self-esteem and offers guidelines for this particular story. A suggested reading list is provided at the end of this section for anyone who would like to explore the themes of self-esteem, emotional literacy, story-telling or group work with children in more depth.

Part 2 holds the story and offers suggestions for discussion topics which can be used to expand on the various elements of self-esteem covered in each chapter.

In Part 3 you will find a selection of activity sheets together with guidelines for using these with groups or with individual children.

2

The Nature of Story-Telling

Why use story-telling to help build healthy self-esteem?

Story-telling of one sort or another is part of the tradition of every culture, capturing the multi-faceted complexities of our lives in a way that speaks to all ages and on many different levels of understanding. Stories have the potential to absorb our attention and fire our imagination; to enrich our learning and to inspire creativity of thought. This is perhaps particularly true of oral stories (including those read either silently or aloud) where the images are 'painted' with words but it is up to the individual as to how they actually experience these in their imagination.

How many of us had a favourite story that we loved to hear or read for ourselves again and again as a young child? Perhaps it reminded us of our own hopes or fears at that time, reflecting in some way the situation in which we found ourselves, the friendships we were forming or losing, the emotions we were struggling to understand. Or perhaps the situations and experiences conveyed in the story were unfamiliar to us but offered a new hope – the potential for things to be different, of new possibilities, of young or vulnerable characters being able to build confidence and skills or call on appropriate help to overcome great adversities.

The appeal of such stories lies in the universal language they employ – the language of imagination – where anything is possible, even if it defies logic. In stories we can readily accept that an animal can talk or a tree can uproot itself and set out on a journey or a small child can outwit a monster.

By the time they are seven (and often younger) most children can comfortably engage with such flights of imagination and safely return again to everyday reality. At some level children of this age can also connect with the metaphorical meaning of fantastical events and through metaphor they are able to explore and deepen their understanding of themselves and the world.

This level of connection is often beyond anything that can be verbalised by the child – they do not need to attempt literal interpretations of the metaphors, they simply experience shifts in perception through the medium of images.

It is also at about the age of six or seven that children generally become more able to cope with longer stories that can be read over an extended period rather than at one encounter. In parallel with their rapidly developing linguistic ability to relate their own 'life-story' sequences, they can carry a story in their minds and pick up the threads again at a later point. They are able to become more actively involved in the process of a story and reflect on the content in order to make predictions about what might happen next, make comparisons, draw conclusions and make judgements. Just as in everyday learning, if their curiosity is aroused by a story then they will make creative connections, ask imaginative questions and actively seek solutions to story problems. This, in turn, will help them to generalise their personal learning from stories into real life more easily because they will have had experience of 'exercising' their imagination.

Imaginative exploration of fictional situations and characters can help children to understand and experience their own emotions more fully and to talk about these in a safe way without fear of 'getting it wrong' or being overwhelmed by their feelings. Such explorations highlight the fact that emotions are a natural part of each of us and that we can experience an emotion even when we don't have the words to describe it.

Through stories children can also begin to understand other people's feelings and points of view and to consider events and situations from a range of different perspectives.

On another very functional level, the use of story-telling on a regular basis encourages the development of listening skills. Children who usually find it difficult to engage in the learning process will often sit for lengthy periods of time absorbed by the rhythm and content of an appropriately chosen story where they may have previously been distractible or anxious during other tasks.

Finally, oral stories that include an interactive element can provide a 'jumping off' point for children to tell their own stories and for these stories to be heard and accepted in a safe and supportive way. Children can be encouraged to recognise that, as well as the ability to produce new and imaginative stories, they each have their own 'life' story to tell and that their unique story is as important as anyone else's.

For all these reasons, the non-competitive nature of story-telling makes it an ideal vehicle for aiding the development and maintenance of healthy self-esteem.

The 'art' of the story-teller

During my years as a therapist I have been privileged to hear many parents, teachers and other therapists telling stories in ways that have children so absorbed that you would think they were in a trance, or so caught up in the adventure that they are desperate to ask questions or will shout out or laugh aloud or wriggle incessantly in their excitement. There have also been some occasions when I have heard a tired or stressed adult read from a book at breakneck speed or with little intonation. Unfortunately, in these instances, the specialness of time spent together in story-telling seemed to be lost, and the children's interest quickly vanished.

My own early attempts at reading short stories in a therapy group of very active boys aged eight to eleven reminded me that there is indeed an 'art' to story-telling or, as one of my nieces once pointed out to me there is an 'art and soul' to it! The art, I discovered, comes partly from tuning in to the mood and needs of the story-listeners and tuning out of any concerns that I, the story-teller, may have about my ability to tell stories. It also comes from tuning in to the story itself and enjoying the variety of rhythm and language that different stories have to offer. When the narrator connects with both the listeners and the story in this way and is able to relax into the 'process' of the story then there is a potential depth in oral story-telling which goes a long way beyond the content of the narrative. This is the 'soul' part.

On a surface level this connection is quickly conveyed to the children. The story-teller suggests by her posture, volume, tone of voice, gesture, facial expression and general rate of speech how 'engaged' she is with both the story and the listeners and how much 'weight' might be accorded to a partic-ular story event or character. Story rituals (see later) also aid the process as does careful preparation and, in some instances, thoughtful selection of props.

So, the role of the story-teller is to 'hold' a story temporarily in safe-keeping and to offer it to the story-listeners in manageable portions. In the language of metaphor I have chosen to think of this process as being like the baking and sharing of a special bread or cake. Some children may eagerly devour large chunks; others take only a morsel, or refuse just now because they're not ready to eat this flavour. Others may take some out of politeness. Yet others take slices and 'squirrel' them away for future feasting. And there will be some who will come back for second and third and fourth helpings before moving on to something else.

The story-teller knows when it is the right time to bring out a familiar offering or to create a new recipe; and with his or her natural baking ability can encourage children to make their own feast – be it a mud pie, rich fruit loaf, wholemeal biscuit, sticky toffee pudding or delicate sponge cake!

The ingredients of this particular tin tortoise cake have been provided for you, and the cake is partially baked. Its final baking and decoration are for you, the story-teller, to complete in your own way – savour the moment!

3

The Nature of Healthy Self-Esteem

Self-esteem is about liking and approving of ourselves. It is about being able to recognise our competencies and accept our need to continue to learn and develop. Building self-esteem is not, however, about strengthening our own self-liking to the detriment of others. This is why we need to place emphasis on building *healthy* self-esteem. Supporting children in this task involves helping them to 'get along in the world': it involves taking into account the personal and social context in which each child operates.

We can view healthy self-esteem as being founded on seven key elements (Plummer 2001). As a child grows and develops, some of these elements may become more central to his or her feelings of self-worth and competency than others but, like an intricate interlocking puzzle, all of them are needed to some degree. The relationship is reciprocal: healthy levels of self-esteem help to strengthen and develop the foundation elements.

The seven elements are outlined below. These are slightly revised and extended versions of the explanations in my earlier books.

Self-knowledge

This is about finding out who 'I' am and where I fit into the social world around me.

- Understanding differences and commonalities – for example, how I am different from others in looks and character, or how I can have an interest or aim in common with others.

- Knowing that I can sometimes behave in different ways according to the situation that I'm in and that I have many aspects to my personality.

- Developing and maintaining my personal values.

- Developing a sense of my personal history – my own 'story'.

Self and others

- Understanding the joys and challenges of relationships. This includes learning to co-operate with others, being able to see things from another person's perspective and developing an understanding of how they might see me, and learning respect and tolerance for other people's views.

- Developing and maintaining my own identity as a separate person while still recognising the natural *inter*dependence of relationships and developing a sense of my family/cultural 'story'.

- Understanding my emotions and being aware of the ways in which I express them. For healthy self-esteem I will need to develop a degree of emotional 'resilience' so that I am not overwhelmed by my emotions and so that I can tolerate frustration. I will need to know that I can choose *how* to express emotions appropriately rather than deny or repress them or act in an inappropriate way. Similarly, I need to be able to recognise other people's emotions and be able to distinguish my feelings from those of others.

Self-acceptance

- Knowing my own strengths and recognising areas that I find difficult and may want to work on. This includes accepting that it is natural to make mistakes and that this is sometimes how we learn best.

- Feeling OK about my physical body.

Self-reliance

- Knowing how to take care of myself, both physically and emotionally: developing an understanding that life is often difficult but there are lots of things that I can do to help myself along the path.

- Building a measure of independence and self-motivation: being able to self-monitor and adjust my actions, feelings and thoughts according to realistic assessments of my progress, and believing that I have mastery over my life and can meet challenges as and when they arise.

Self-expression

- Understanding how we communicate with each other. This involves learning to 'read the signals' beyond the words so that I can understand others more successfully and also express myself more fully and congruently.

- Developing creativity in self-expression and recognising and celebrating the unique ways in which we each express who we are.

Self-confidence

- Knowing that my opinions, thoughts and actions have value and that I have the right to express them.

- Developing my knowledge and abilities so that I feel able to experiment with different methods of problem-solving and can be flexible enough to alter my strategies if needed.

- Being able to accept challenges and make choices.

- Being secure enough in myself to be able to cope successfully with the unexpected.

Self-awareness

- Developing the ability to be focused in the here and now rather than absorbed in negative thoughts about the past or future. This includes an awareness of my feelings as they arise.

- Understanding that emotional, mental and physical changes are a natural part of my life and that I have choices about *how* I change and develop.

The story of the little tin tortoise aims to explore a variety of issues linked to the early stages of development of these elements. Because of their inter-relatedness the themes run throughout the story. There is, however, a slightly different focus for each chapter, allowing for more in-depth exploration of particular elements at different points.

4

Guidelines for Sharing the Story

Preparation

In order for each story-telling session to run as smoothly as possible, it is worth taking time to prepare yourself and the physical environment before-hand. This doesn't have to be an elaborate preparation but may involve gathering a few props (see later), making sure that you have a glass of water handy and ensuring that your chosen story area is comfortable and inviting.

Throughout the story there are opportunities to engage children in talking about various events and emotions. You will need to allow plenty of time for this discussion when you are planning your story-telling session. You may find it helpful to read through the chapters in advance so that you can gauge how much time to allow and which questions you might want to focus on for the particular needs of your child or group. You may want to read a whole chapter at a time or only part of a chapter, depending on your assess-ment of group or individual abilities with regard to concentration and taking part.

It is also important to give careful consideration to what you believe to be appropriate 'listening' behaviour since this may be different for story-telling sessions as compared to other shared activities. At home, story-telling may involve being cuddled up together, perhaps wrapped in a story blanket (see below). In a group situation some children, for example those who have a language disorder and who may have done specific work on listening tasks, need to know that story-telling involves a *different* sort of listening and that there are therefore some different behaviours that are acceptable. For example a child might be colouring a picture while listening to a story, she might have her eyes closed, she might choose to sit on the floor or even to lie down. Some children may still be listening intently even if they are fidgeting. You will need to decide what you feel is acceptable in terms of these differences within a given group and how you will acknowledge and facilitate this so that other children are not distracted. Although this might seem very obvious, the important point is that if the story-teller notices 'unusual' listening behaviours and is preoccupied by a desire to control these, then the 'magic' of a story can easily be lost.

Non-judgemental acceptance

The questions posed to children during and after each chapter are not specifically designed to test their understanding of the story or their level of emotional awareness, although of course, levels of understanding will soon become apparent. Such interactions do, however, provide a safe context for children to talk about how they feel and what they think.

This is an opportunity for making it clear to children that their ideas are valued, that they will be listened to and that the story-teller appreciates their growing awareness and knowledge. A relaxed, non-competitive interaction should be encouraged in order to give children the freedom of choice about how much or how little they will contribute or take from the story.

Group support

Just as in any other group, where two or more children are involved in a story-telling session they will need to have clear guidelines about appropriate interaction. The most important aspect of this is to ensure that everyone is aware of how to give positive feedback to each other and listen to each other's ideas in a non-judgemental way. Children need to know beforehand that there are no right or wrong answers where story-telling is concerned and that all ideas and contributions will be respected. Within this framework they can question another child's views or ask him to say a bit more about what he is thinking in relation to the story event or character. However, it is obviously not acceptable for children to make judgemental comments. You may find it useful to give clear examples of what is and is not acceptable before you start the story.

Using props

Children do not need to be able to see the pages of this story while you are reading since the idea is for the teller to use his or her own enjoyment of story-telling to engage the interest of the listeners. However, in recognition of the fact that some young children, as well as older children with learning disabilities, do benefit from concrete ways to access story material, a set of black and white illustrations has been provided (Appendix D). These could perhaps be coloured and laminated and added to the display area at the end of the session.

You may also want to consider using appropriate toys, puppets or pictures collected by you and the children as the story progresses. These can be set up in a designated area that then becomes the 'story place' – the place where you sit to tell the story and where children can add their contributions to the story process as and when appropriate.

Story rituals

Achieving a balance between the discussions (the logical learning) and the magic of story can be challenging. One of the joys of stories is that they do not need to be interpreted and analysed by adults in order for most children to be able to draw on their meaning. In fact, too much analysis of the meaning of what is happening in a story can diminish the power of the words and images and may actually hinder a child's ability to learn from these. However, *joint exploration* of the themes provides a rich context in which children can learn important life skills. One way of achieving this balance is to incorporate story rituals into the process. Such rituals help children to appreciate the difference between fantasy and reality and also help them to feel safe and 'contained'. They can then more easily 'settle into' a story and participate at whatever level is appropriate for their needs at the time. You may want to experiment with a combination of the following ideas. You will quickly discover which ones work most successfully both for you as a story-teller and for the child or children in your 'audience'.

Use the magic of silence to mark the beginning and end of each story-telling session. Allow silence to 'arrive' at the start of this special time together and then invite the story to join your story circle. This can be done in a number of ways. You might simply say 'I wonder what the tin tortoise story is going to tell us today', or 'Let's sit quietly for a few moments until the story is ready to begin'. You could also use a small bell or other musical instrument to signal the beginning of the listening time after the silence has settled. At the end of the story, sit quietly again before moving away from the story area or initiating any further discussion. A short silence gives children the space for their thoughts and feelings to emerge in a natural way.

Use a story 'mantle' as a regular part of your story-telling routine. This could simply be a piece of cloth, a shawl or a blanket. Putting on a cloak, wrapping yourself in a story blanket or draping your chair with a distinctive piece of material all convey the 'specialness' of a story-telling time. Children can then either use the same cloak or blanket or choose their own when it is their turn to tell a story.

You can also use the moment of putting on the cloak to show the children that we can ask a story how it would like to be told. You might, for example, close your eyes (or give some other appropriate indication that you are concentrating) and say something like 'How would you (or "this story") like to be told today?' Wait for a short while and get a feel for what your child or group need from the story-telling session. You might then tell them such things as 'This story needs to be told very quietly today', or 'it needs to be told outside', 'it wants to be told while everyone is colouring in a picture' or 'it needs to be told in two parts'. You may want to encourage participation by saying, 'This part of the story wants us to join in as much as possible and ask lots of questions' or 'it wants us to start by relaxing/by stretching and moving/with some music'.

In this way, the story process becomes a personalised journey for the children (and for you as the story-teller) and can be structured to meet individual or group needs.

Wherever possible, avoid 'breaking' the story mode during the telling (for example, where you have not specifically asked the children something or you feel that answering a child's question will interrupt the flow too much at that particular point). If you need to respond to an interruption or unexpected question, try responding as the story-teller or from the perspective of one of the characters. You could say something like 'Let's see if the story will tell us the answer to that,' or 'That's just what Coco wanted to know. Let's see if she found the answer.'

Keep in mind any *unanswered* questions that could be explored at the end of the story session either through discussion or through one of the drama techniques outlined in Appendix C. Remembering and acknowledging a child's participation in this way also shows that you take his or her questions seriously and are ready to help with the exploration of possible answers.

Expansion topics

The expansion topics can be used in a variety of different ways to help children to consider and expand their knowledge of themselves and others, and their capacity for personal development.

If you are telling this story at home you will be able to use the topics as part of a regular story-telling routine, perhaps choosing just one discussion point which appeals to both you and your child following the reading of each chapter.

In the classroom, it is possible to incorporate almost all of the expansion topics into areas of the National Curriculum. For example, several of the topics have been linked with the English National Curriculum guidelines for PSHE and Citizenship in Key Stage 1 (see Appendix B). These can also be modified to provide opportunities for more in-depth exploration of relevant issues for Year 3 pupils (Key Stage 2). A number of the topics can be adapted to meet targets for the National Literacy Strategy (speaking and listening; reading and writing) and many of the discussion points lend themselves to the use of key drama techniques such as 'hot seating' and 'tunnel of thoughts' (see Appendix C for an explanation of these techniques).

Naturally, it is not anticipated that teachers will want to use the story to cover all these objectives. They are offered as a reference point for those who wish to select relevant objectives for use over a period of one half-term or more.

Counsellors and therapists from a variety of disciplines will also be able to draw on the ideas presented throughout the story to expand on particular issues of self-esteem relevant to individuals and groups of children, embedding the discussions and activities within their own particular therapeutic framework.

Using the activity sheets

The activity sheets are intended as an adjunct to discussions in pairs and groups. Most of these are adapted and extended versions of a selection of activity sheets from *Helping Children to Build Self-Esteem* (Plummer 2001). However, please keep in mind that the learning emphasis of this current book is very much to do with *sharing* and *talking* about a story. Activity sheets can be a very useful tool in many situations but they do need to be used carefully and in a structured way. The aim here is to encourage children to work together rather than to sit quietly completing a written sheet on their own. This sharing and talking can be a highly effective and motivating way of learning for most children. It also, of course, helps to foster effective use and understanding of social communication, providing opportunities for encouraging collaborative, respectful relationships. This in turn further contributes to the building of healthy self-esteem.

So, while a variety of activity sheets are offered for each chapter the guideline is always 'less is more'. Several slow-paced sessions using only one, or perhaps two activity sheets at a time, can give room for children to be far more creative in their thinking and problem-solving than one fast-paced session involving several activities. And of course, some children will gain more from the story by simply listening to it than by completing any type of activity sheet at all!

Suggestions for further reading

Antidote (2003) *The Emotional Literacy Handbook: Promoting Whole-School Strategies*. London: David Fulton Publishers.

Dwivedi, K.N. (ed.) (1997) *The Therapeutic Use of Stories*. London and New York: Routledge.

Dwivedi, K.N. (ed.) (1999) *Group Work with Children and Adolescents: A Handbook*. London: Jessica Kingsley Publishers.

Glouberman, D. (2003) *Life Choices, Life Changes: Develop Your Personal Vision with Imagework*. London: Hodder and Stoughton.

Hillman, J. (2002) *Healing Fiction*. Putnam, Connecticut: Spring Publications, Inc.

Jennings, C. (1992) *Children as Story-tellers: Developing Language Skills in the Classroom*. Melbourne: Oxford University Press.

Mellon, N. (2002) *Storytelling with Children*. Stroud: Hawthorn Press.

Murphy, C. (2000) *PSHE Through Fiction*. Cambridgeshire PSHE Service.

Paley, V.G. (1991) *The Boy Who Would Be a Helicopter*. London: Harvard University Press.

Plummer, D. (1999) *Using Interactive Imagework with Children: Walking on the Magic Mountain*. London: Jessica Kingsley Publishers.

Plummer, D. (2001) *Helping Children to Build Self-Esteem: A Photocopiable Activities Book*. London: Jessica Kingsley Publishers.

Sunderland, M. (2000) *Using Story Telling as a Therapeutic Tool with Children*. Bicester: Speechmark Publishing Ltd.

Tyrrell, J. (2001) *The Power of Fantasy in Early Learning*. London and New York: Routledge.

The Adventures
of the Little Tin Tortoise

1

Waking Up

I would like to share a story with you. It is a story of adventure and discovery; a story about finding your way in the world. It is a story that my father told to me and his father told to him before that, and my grandfather's mother told to my grandfather when he was a child. It is a special story about a long time ago and yet it only happened yesterday and today. Or may be it will happen tomorrow – and that is its magic! Are you ready to discover this story? Is this a good time for you? Then let's look and listen quietly as it spreads itself out for us. Gently, very gently it unfolds and lets us see all its different parts.

And this is the first part.

There was a special time – just the right time for such a thing to happen – when an old man made a little tin tortoise. I don't know the name of the man and I think this is sad because I would like to be able to tell you whom the little tin tortoise first belonged to, but there – story-tellers don't always know everything! What I *do* know is that this man was quite tall and not very stout and had quite remarkable brown eyes that sparkled when he talked. He was a tinsmith and he made tin watering cans and cooking pots and tin plates and bowls in a small store on a busy street in a little town called Bambous.

'I haven't heard of Bambous,' I can hear you say. And indeed I am not surprised at this! But let me tell you that it is a town on the beautiful island of Mauritius which rests in the turquoise and sapphire blue waters of the Indian Ocean.

Well, the old man's store was called 'Tin Treasures'. It was made of great sheets of corrugated metal and it was one of many stores that had been built in a row along the main street of Bambous. 'Tin Treasures' had a blue roof and its metal window shutters and doors were painted bright yellow. The old man had worked in his store for many years and everyone in the town of Bambous knew him and came to him to buy their kitchenware. They would look along the shelves and the workbench piled high with shiny tin goods and if they were in the mood for spending some rupees they would choose just the right sized bowls or pots or plates for their particular needs at that particular time.

Often they would linger for a while and talk with the old man about what was happening in the town or what good and bad things had happened in their family since they had last visited the store. Sometimes they talked about the plans for the next festival or town celebration. The old man liked to talk with his customers in this way. If they asked him for advice about family matters or personal decisions he would pause in the middle of his work and take time to think very carefully about what to say. He believed that people get on best in the world if they can work out problems for themselves but sometimes he also had very wise advice to give that would help them on their way.

Well, I think that one day, a day when he didn't have many customers to talk with, the old man just got really bored with making pots and bowls and plates and watering cans and he thought to himself that it would be fun to make a tortoise, and so he did!

He took a great sheet of tin from the back of his store (it was enough tin to have made at least two good strong bowls) and he cut out a circle. He beat and hammered and recut the circle of tin until it was shaped like a tortoise shell and then he used a chisel to make the shapes on the shell that all tortoises have – shapes like patchwork hexagons – you know that shape? Then, just to make the shell look *extra* special, and because he was particularly enjoying making the tortoise, he carved some delicate patterns in three of the hexagons.

Then the old man cut another piece of tin to make a body for the tortoise and he beat it and hammered it to make one end into the head and the other end into a tiny tail. He made two little dents in the tin for eyes and two more for ears and two tiny ones for nostrils and a line for the mouth. Then he made a flat circle for the underneath of the tortoise and he took a very hot soldering iron and he stuck all the pieces together. All the time he was working he smiled and hummed to himself because he was feeling happy.

When he had finished he looked at the tortoise on his workbench and he wondered if he should give it a name. There were some giant tortoises in a special park not far from Bambous but they didn't have names. They had big white numbers painted on their shells instead. Perhaps some of the keepers had given the giant tortoises proper names as well but visitors didn't know about this. The old man liked to think so! *Can you think of some good tortoise names?*

In the store it was nearly five o'clock and the old man was thinking about his journey home and how his bicycle needed some repairs. He should really have taken it to the bicycle repair store instead of making a tortoise, and now he had two less bowls to sell in his store and his wife would not be pleased.

Do you know how it feels when you spend a long time doing something and then when it's finished you feel a little sad or disappointed when you thought you would feel really happy? Well that's how the man felt.

So in the end there was no name given and the man shut up his store and went away feeling less happy than when he had started to make the tin tortoise. The street outside the store was already noisy with people hurrying home and the old man felt the heat of the long day sitting heavily across his brow.

Now I should tell you that when the store had closed and everything was in darkness it was the usual custom for the pots and pans and plates and bowls to rattle and shake and stretch themselves and check on who was new in the store and who had been sold. They would guess at where 'pot number 33' had gone or why 'plate 1020' had been rejected by a customer when plates 1019 and 1021 had both been sold. There was always a lot of noise. It really is a wonder that no-one ever heard what went on after the man had gone home. Well on this particular evening, all this noise woke the tin tortoise with a start. To be honest he found it rather frightening and so for a while he kept his eyes closed and tried very hard not to move.

Gradually he realised that his body was hurting from being still for so long and so he slowly began to stretch a little. He stretched out his body as far as it would go and he stretched out his neck as far as that would go. He opened one eye but he couldn't see anything. He opened the other eye but he still couldn't see anything. All he could hear was the loud chattering around him. So he waited and waited and gradually, really ever so slowly, he started to be able to see in the semi-darkness and gradually, ever so slowly, he began to understand what he was hearing.

'So – that's six new plates and one new bowl then,' rattled a very large saucepan.

'Much fewer than usual,' squeaked a battered looking soup bowl.

'Ah!' sighed the saucepan. 'He doesn't work as fast as he used to. He's lost the spark that kept him working hard.'

'It's since his son and grandson moved away,' said the bowl, as if this was a great secret that he was revealing.

'Yes indeed.' The saucepan creaked and sighed again. It had been in the store for a very long time – slightly damaged and too large for most people to need, it was now used for display purposes only. Still, that meant that it was in charge of the store when the man was away. Now it wanted to check the newcomers.

'So – let's see if these plates and this bowl are up to the usual standard then. Come here plates so I can see you better.'

The plates flipped onto their edge and each rolled past the saucepan for inspection. 'Good, good, yes not bad, in need of a bit of polishing, excellent workmanship. Mmm – not quite as smooth as you could be.'

Each plate listened anxiously to its assessment and wondered how this would affect its chances of being sold.

'Now bowl – come here where I can see you – my eyesight isn't what it used to be.'

The tin tortoise looked around the store and waited for the new bowl to roll its way to the saucepan. But nothing moved.

'I'm waiting – what's the matter?'

Still nothing moved.

The tin tortoise thought that the saucepan sounded angry and so he started to draw his head back into his shell very slowly and quietly so he could hide. Suddenly – thwack! He felt the hard edge of a frying pan handle across his shell.

'What are you doing waiting here?' said the frying pan. 'You must go to be inspected.'

Then the tortoise realised with great consternation that the saucepan thought he was a bowl! 'Oh no,' he wanted to shout 'I'm a tortoise not a bowl.'

He stuck out his head again and tried to speak these words. At first only a little squeak came out of his mouth.

'What's that?' rattled the saucepan loudly. 'What did you say?'

The tortoise tried again. He struggled to find his voice and his little tin head shook with the effort.

'Tortle,' he said at last.

The pots and plates around him began to laugh.

'Tortle,' said the little tortoise. Then gathering all his tin strength he took a deep breath and said, 'Tortoise – I'm not a bowl. I'm a tortoise!' The sound of his voice so surprised him that he felt quite shaken and immediately pulled his head back into his shell again!

Well, I'm sorry to say that the whole store full of pots and pans and plates and bowls laughed and laughed and laughed. They rattled and shook and coughed and spluttered as the little tortoise peered at them from inside his shell. Poor little tortoise – he felt sad and angry and lonely and confused all at once, but because he had never felt any of these feelings before, he just knew that he felt horrible inside.

At last the big saucepan banged its handle on the shelf where it was resting.

'Stop! Stop now!' it said, composing itself once more and taking a deep breath to prevent itself from laughing. When the store had quietened down it said in a much more gentle voice, 'Come little bowl. I can see now that you are a very unusual bowl – the man has given you a decoration and two handles. He has given you a lid where none of the other bowls in here have lids! But you can't possibly be a tortoise little one – you have no legs!'

The new plates all sniggered and the saucepan banged its handle down again impatiently to silence them. 'You see little bowl, tortoises have legs to help them to move around. If you were a tortoise you would have four legs. The man only makes cooking pots and pans and bowls and plates here. You are definitely and most absolutely *not* a tortoise.'

Well – can you imagine what that little tortoise felt like then? He knew without any doubt at all that he most definitely and absolutely *was* a tortoise. To be mistaken for a bowl was bad enough but to be mistaken for a bowl because the person who made you had forgotten to give you legs – that must have been a very sad discovery. The little tin tortoise shrank further and further into his shell. The big old saucepan sighed heavily. It could not think of anything else to say that might help the new bowl to feel better about itself.

The pots and pans and plates and bowls settled into their places on the shelves and once again the store fell into silence. It was not a comfortable silence. Each one of them was thinking about how a little bowl could possibly imagine that it could be a tortoise. The plates could not understand it at all because they were very happy to be what they were. But I think that some of the pots and pans and bowls would have liked to have been something different too. Maybe there was a bowl that wished it could be a cooking pot for a day. Maybe there was a pot that wished it could be a pink pigeon. Have you ever imagined what it would be like if you weren't who you are?

And so this is the end of the first part of this story. We will leave the store in its quiet state for now and we will leave our thoughts with the little tortoise, tucked up in his shell. *What thoughts and wishes would you like to give him to help him to sleep a little?*

Expansion topics

- Talk about the thoughts and feelings that would be helpful to leave with the little tortoise as he falls asleep.

- How do you think the old man was feeling?

- The little tortoise felt lots of different emotions but he didn't know what they were called. Collect 'feeling' words together and talk about different times that people might feel different emotions. **Activity sheets 1 and 2**.

- Everything in the store believed that the tortoise was a bowl. Has anyone ever called you by the wrong name? What would you feel if someone made a mistake about who you are or what you have done or haven't done? When would that be OK? When would it not be OK?

- Some of the pots and pans and bowls wondered what it would be like to be something different. If you were an animal, what animal would you be? What would you call yourself? Why?

- The plates were laughing at the little tortoise and this upset him. Is there a difference between teasing and bullying? What does it feel like to be teased? How can you deal with teasing? **Activity sheets 3 and 4**.

- Where is Mauritius? What would it be like to live in a different country? What would you like/not like about being in a different place? What sort of things do you think would be the same/different?

2

Thoughts and Feelings

Now we've arrived at the second part of our story. Do you remember, we left the little tortoise tucked up in his shell inside the store? You and I left him some kind thoughts and wishes to help him to sleep and I think that he *did* sleep a little because, although he was sad, he was also hopeful that the new day would be better for him.

And now the old man has arrived on his bicycle and he has unlocked the big yellow metal doors and the big yellow metal window shutters. It is already very hot, even though it is only early in the morning, and the old man moves slowly because his body is not as strong and flexible as it used to be. He pulls back the large doors to let some light into the store and now we can see all the things that he has made lined up on the long shelves and on his workbench. Here is the tin tortoise who has remembered just in time to put his head out from his shell before the old man sees him. He really does look like an upturned bowl doesn't he?

The old man smiles when he sees his work from the day before. He is feeling more cheerful again today and he thinks that it will be a good day for selling his tinware. He sets out the large saucepan and a few other display items at the front of his store and collects up the six plates that he made yesterday. He thinks that maybe his memory is getting even worse than usual because he is sure that he stacked these plates in a pile before he left last night.

'That nuisance cat must have been in here again,' he says aloud (since he doesn't want to think about growing older and getting forgetful).

He carefully selects a new sheet of tin ready for the next batch of plates and begins his day's work. The saucepan sighs quietly with relief – it really must remember to get the store in order again before the man arrives each morning but with so much to think about these days and with advancing age…well, let's just say that its memory is also not quite as sharp as it used to be!

And so the day passes. The tortoise sits on the workbench and watches the man crafting the new plates. He really wants to ask the man to make him some legs but the saucepan has already warned him that he must not speak to the man or he will lose his voice for ever. 'Now bowl,' he had whispered early this morning, 'We don't speak to humans EVER. You must understand this. It would scare some humans to hear the noises that we make. Others would throw us away, thinking that our metal was faulty. Either way, you would never be able to speak again – it's a rule that cannot be broken.' The tin tortoise has a great fear of losing his voice, having only just found it, so he is determined to stay quiet today even though he really, desperately wants to ask for some legs.

Sometimes when people come into the store he feels a little nervous and he wants to pull his head back inside his shell but he remembers that he must not move either so he has to be brave and keep very still. And so the day passes and the little tortoise has plenty of time to think and to listen and to watch. For a while, he thinks about what it is like to be a tortoise with no legs. He knew from the moment that he first 'woke up' yesterday that he was a tortoise but he had not realised that he should have legs until the saucepan had told him.

This was another feeling to learn about – this feeling of 'what if?' What if he had never known that he needed legs? There were no other tortoises in the store with which to compare himself. If the saucepan hadn't pointed out his incompleteness then perhaps he would be quite happy to be the way that he is. But now he feels a strange discontent. He has a sensation in his body and in his head that is very uncomfortable – a bit like the feelings he had yesterday but mixed up with these thoughts of 'what if?'… 'What if I *did* have legs,' he thinks, 'How would things be different? Would the old man like me more? Would someone come and buy me and take me home? Would I be more handsome or less handsome? Would the pots and pans and plates at last believe that I *am* a tortoise and not a bowl with a lid that doesn't open? Would they be kind to me or would they be unkind and not want to speak to me because I am different from them? A tortoise doesn't belong in a store that sells pots and pans,' thinks the little tortoise sadly.

After a while he starts trying to think of a way to change this sad feeling. 'What if I pretend that I really believe I *am* a bowl? Would the others accept me and like me? But then that would be hard because I like being a tortoise. What if…? What if…?' All these thoughts go round and round in the little tortoise's head until he feels quite dizzy and more and more bewildered. In the end he decides that it is all too confusing and he tries to concentrate very hard on what is going on around him instead, hoping that this will help him to feel a little better.

The first thing that he notices is that the storekeeper has lots of visitors during the day and that sometimes these visitors don't buy anything – they simply stand and talk with the old man while he carries on working. Occasionally someone brings in something that needs mending – a pan with a loose handle or a plate that needs some dents smoothing out. The big saucepan has told the little tortoise that the old man knows that his customers could very easily do this mending themselves, but he always obliges because he knows that they have really come to talk about other things.

Today, however, the old man says very little to his customers and they leave quite quickly, wondering what is the matter with the storekeeper and whether or not they should enquire after his health or just leave him alone. Like the little tortoise, he is also very deep in his own thoughts for most of the day.

The little tortoise soon notices that there are creatures who visit the store as well. They seem to pass unnoticed by the man. A pale gecko scurries across the floor and climbs the wall to sit for a while behind some pots. A mynah bird hops into the entrance way and has a look around before hopping out again. Then, late in the afternoon, a man brings his daughter to the store. There is a yellow dog following closely on the little girl's heels but it stops at the entrance and sits facing into the store – as still as a statue, watching closely. The girl scans the shelves in the store while her father talks to the old man. The little tortoise notices her long dark hair hanging in a thick plait that swings from side to side as she moves her head. Then all at once she comes close to the workbench, bobs down so that her chin is resting on the rough wooden surface and says, 'Hello little tortoise.'

Well – can you imagine such a thing happening? The little tortoise smiles right deep down inside and, although he really wants to laugh and shout because someone has at last realised that he is not a bowl, he remembers the saucepan's warning and just looks really hard right into the little girl's eyes. She is smiling at him and with one finger she gently strokes the top of his head.

Now her father has finished talking with the old man and he calls his daughter to his side. As they leave, she turns and gives a little wave to the tortoise. The old man is already busy working again and he doesn't notice this happen. He bends his head low and wipes a tear from his eye – the little girl and her father remind him so much of his own son and grandson who moved away to England. But outside in the street the yellow dog has seen and heard everything.

Expansion topics

- Talk about 'what if' everyone in the world was exactly the same. What might be good about this? What might not be so good? What is good about having things in common with others? **Activity sheets 5 and 6**.

- Have you ever thought about what it would be like to be someone else? First think about what it is like to be you. Then think what it would be like to be someone else for a day. **Activity sheets 7 and 8**.

- Talk about how feelings can change from one moment to the next. What sorts of things help you to feel happy? **Activity sheets 9 and 10**.

- The little tortoise drew his head into his shell when he felt anxious or nervous. How do we show that we are feeling anxious? How do we show that we are feeling angry or happy? **Activity sheet 11**.

3

Making a Decision

Today, the third part of the little tortoise story has come to find us. I'm sorry to say that I forgot to tell you a most important thing that happened after the little girl and her father left the store; or maybe this part of the story wanted to be told today – I'm not really sure. But anyway I'm going to tell you now.

So, when the old man finally looked up from his work he realised that it was once again time to go home. He had been deep in sad remembrance while he was working but now he caught sight of the little tortoise sitting on his workbench. He heaved a very heavy sigh and picked up the tortoise, turned it around in his work-worn hands and examined it from all angles. He sighed again. He ran a finger over the shell and wiped away a smudge of dirt. 'Your shell is very beautiful' he said out loud. 'I think Sandeep would have enjoyed playing with you.' He held the tortoise for a long time just looking at him silently and the little tortoise felt the heaviness in the old man's heart.

Let's just pause here for a moment. I wonder if you can guess how the old man was feeling. What might he have been thinking about? What do you think he did next?

Well – let's see if you are right.

The old man laid the tortoise down again – not on the workbench this time but on a high shelf with lots of bits of twisted tin – left over scraps that would eventually be recycled.

'Tomorrow it's back to normal,' said the old man sharply. 'I'm thinking too much about things that I can't change. No more tortoise projects.'

He sounded angry, his voice harsh and loud. He moved purposefully around the store, bringing in the pots and pans from outside, putting his tools away and emptying his tin cash box of the few rupees that he had taken that day. He had left the store and locked the door behind him in a matter of only a few moments. Before the closing door brought darkness to the store, the little tortoise briefly saw that there were huge dark clouds gathering in the sky and he could hear rain beginning to fall on the metal roof. The air was full of the warm heaviness of a breaking storm mixed with the sweet smell of the damp earth.

Now the little tortoise was abandoned high on a shelf and was feeling very sad. He was afraid that it was his fault that the man was so angry and unhappy. His time so far in this world had been full of many different feelings. It was so confusing being a tin tortoise in such a place. He really didn't understand what was happening.

When you are a tin tortoise you do not measure your days by hours and minutes like some people do. Instead you measure them by events and feelings. This little tortoise had certainly felt many different feelings and his days had been full of many different sights and sounds and happenings. It seemed to him that he had been in the store for a very long time. And now things were about to happen that would require all the courage that our little friend could gather.

As soon as the man had closed the door the pots and watering cans and plates and bowls all started talking at once. In fact, some of them were shouting, they were so eager to be heard. The store sounded like a train station or a great factory with all the banging and clattering of the tin. It was lucky that the storm outside was gathering force and the rain was now beating so heavily on the metal roof that it drowned out some of the noise from inside.

The big saucepan took charge again. It banged its handle on the work-bench and called the store to order. It had to wait a short while for everything to go quiet because some of the plates still whispered as if no one could hear them. Eventually there was silence and the little tortoise, feeling a bit braver, put his head out from his shell. He blinked a few times until his eyes got used to the semi-darkness. He soon realised that everything in the store was looking at him. The saucepan coughed.

'Now, it seems to me that we have an apology to make to you, little tortoise, because indeed that is what you are – a tortoise with a patterned shell and not a bowl at all.'

The plates flapped up and down on the shelves and chorused, 'Yes. Yes – a tortoise, not a bowl, no, not a bowl at all!'

The little tortoise stretched his head out just a tiny bit further.

'AND,' continued the saucepan grandly 'Not withstanding the aforementioned fact it beholds me to…' At which point he broke off to scold a plate that had developed a fit of the giggles. 'Ahem. Well, as I was saying, it's my duty to call a meeting of the Council to decide what should be done.'

'Done?' said the little tortoise, 'Must something be done?'

'Oh yes – indeed, indeed something must be done,' chorused the plates.

The big saucepan coughed again and looked at the plates sternly. Then it rapped its handle on the bench very deliberately and slowly three times. The plates and bowls and pans shuffled and jostled uneasily but no longer spoke. The little tortoise could feel himself holding his breath in expectation. He didn't have to wait long. Through an opening in the corner of the store came a sleek white cat, closely followed by a mynah bird, slapping his yellow feet against the floor and looking to left and right with quick, darting movements of his head. After another short wait a lean, golden yellow dog squeezed through the opening. Once inside the store she turned and barked through the hole, 'Stay there until I've finished. Don't move and don't talk to any strangers'. Then she nodded to the group. 'I'm sorry to be last here. The pups were late back from beach patrol lessons.'

'Welcome Saffron,' replied the saucepan. 'Don't worry, the others have only just arrived. Spanner will you fill Saffron in on the situation so far.'

'Of course,' purred the cat and began to speak to Saffron in a quiet voice, too quiet for the little tortoise to hear what was being said.

So the cat, the mynah bird and the dog formed a solemn half circle in front of the workbench. The little tortoise waited to find out what would happen. This was a difficult time and he was getting very nervous. He wondered if they would decide to make him leave because he didn't belong here. This frightened him greatly because he had only a vague idea of what lay beyond the doors of the store and it had all seemed very busy and noisy – it would surely be very easy for a little tortoise with no legs to be trampled on if he left the safety of the store.

Have you ever worried about something even when you didn't know for sure whether or not it was going to happen? Sometimes when we think about something from the past or the future it can feel as though it is happening right now and this is what the tortoise felt like. He was getting more and more frightened and feeling more and more sick just thinking about what *might* happen! Even though he had not really been happy in the store when the man was not there, it was the only place that he knew. And now the big saucepan was being nice to him and he felt safe here. He thought that maybe he could even learn to get along with the laughing plates if he tried hard enough to ignore their teasing.

The Council were talking together in very quiet voices now so he had to concentrate to try and catch what they were saying. Every now and then one of them would ask the assembled pots and pans a general question such as, 'What did the old man say as he was working?' or 'Has he ever made anything different like this before?' and once 'What is your opinion of the old man's state of mind?' The consultation seemed to go on for ever but finally they appeared ready to pronounce their awful judgement.

'Well, little tortoise,' said Saffron, 'We would like to hear your thoughts now'.

The little tortoise felt his throat tighten. 'Oh please,' he managed to whisper, 'Please don't send me away. I can try to be a bowl. Really I can.'

'Goodness me!' came the quick reply from the saucepan. 'We don't want you to try to be anything but what you are. You are a tortoise and should be proud of that. We simply want to know what you propose to do about it.'

'I'm sorry – I don't understand. Do you mean what do I propose to do about being a tortoise?'

Saffron smiled and spoke more softly than before. 'No, small one! What we mean is, what do you propose to do about getting some legs and a name and going out to explore the world?'

'Oh!' thought the little tortoise anxiously, 'I'm too little to have a name and I'm too little and fragile to explore the world. My shell is only made of tin and could so easily be dented.' He must have spoken these words aloud without meaning to because the plates were sniggering again. He felt embarrassed and didn't quite know what to do or where to look. It was unfair of the plates to laugh at him. He couldn't help being scared of the world. Plates knew what their purpose was. They knew they were plates. They knew that someone would buy them and use them to eat their food from. They had nothing to fear in the big world. But a small tin tortoise with a delicate shell – well that was a different matter all together.

The Council members were talking amongst themselves once more. At last Saffron spoke again.

'We would like to help you, small one, and we have a plan. Be quiet, plates! It is rude and undignified to laugh at our new friend. We are concerned that the man may lose interest in his work because you remind him too much of painful things that have happened in his life. He will not make his living if he starts to worry about the past and you will never get your legs if you stay here. Spanner lives with the owners of the bicycle repair store and she thinks that she can get you some legs there. She proposes to take you to the store and the Council agree that this is a good plan. What do you think?'

The little tortoise could hear what Saffron was saying but found it hard to take in all the information. He needed time to think about it all and make what the old man would call 'an informed decision' based on all the evidence. But it seemed he was not to be given the chance. Spanner was anxious to be gone.

'Come on,' she purred. 'If we're going to go we need to leave soon. We won't get all the way to the bicycle repair store tonight as it is. The rain is getting heavier and the journey will be difficult.'

'The rain is getting heavier,' chorused the plates. 'Time to get going. Time to get going'.

But the little tortoise took a deep breath and bravely said, 'This is a lot for me to understand. Please let me have just a very short think so that I can work out what to do.'

The Council were a little shocked at this because they had thought that the little tortoise would simply say 'yes' to their plan. But they all agreed to wait while he had a think about things. The little tortoise drew his head back into his shell as far as it would go and in the dark comfort of this protection he thought carefully about his choices. Should he stay or should he go? *How would you help him to make a decision? What would you do if you were this little tortoise? What would your decision be?*

Well, after a very short while inside his shell the little tortoise had decided what he must do. Although the idea of leaving the store was scary he knew that the Council would help him. He knew now that he wanted to be a tortoise that could move and he knew that he didn't want the old man to be unhappy. And so he found himself coming out from his shell once more and agreeing to the Council's proposal. The Council members nodded in approval and congratulated him on his decision. There was no time to lose. In a flash Spanner had leapt on to the shelf next to him and was patting him with one of her paws, pushing him closer and closer to the edge. One final swipe and he fell to the ground with a loud clatter. It made him feel sick but luckily he landed the right way up so his shell was not damaged! Spanner jumped from the shelf after him and landed lightly by his side. Now Saffron came near and began to push the little tortoise with her nose towards the hole in the corner. She was able to make him slide easily along the floor on his flat underside and he was soon on the other side of the store.

'Farewell, small one,' said the frying pan as the tortoise slid past it. 'Be brave. May your life be full of adventure!'

'Goodbye,' squeaked one of the bowls. 'Be happy.'

'Be happy. Be happy,' rattled the plates in unison.

'Thank you,' gasped the little tortoise.

The big saucepan dipped its handle ever so slightly. 'Take care,' it said gravely. Then, almost as an afterthought, it added, 'Go wisely. Watch for false friends.'

And before he could say anything at all in response to this, the little tortoise found himself pushed through the hole, out into the stormy night and up close to two wet black noses belonging to two mud-covered puppies.

Expansion topics

- Talk about how, when someone is sad, they can sometimes sound or act as though they are angry. Talk about how we can sometimes mix up our feelings. Talk about the effects of different emotions on the body. **Activity sheets 12–14**.

- Use 'thought bubbling' to talk about trying to 'fit in' with a group. What does the little tortoise feel about staying in the store? **Activity sheet 15**.

- How do you make decisions? What helps you to make a decision?

- Use a 'tunnel of thoughts' to explore the little tortoise's dilemma. Should he stay or should he leave the store?

- How do you think the tortoise felt when he was praised for making his decision?

- Talk about asking for/accepting help from teachers, friends and family.

- Talk about how we all sometimes need 'thinking time' on our own. What do different people do when they need 'thinking time'? For example, you might tell someone that you need time to think, spend some time on your own in your bedroom, or do a quiet activity such as drawing, while you are thinking.

4

Making Friends

Today the fourth part of the story about the little tin tortoise has come to say hello. Let's make space for it to spread itself out and share its treasures with us.

So many things have happened since we last saw the little tortoise. While you have been away, going about your daily life, getting things done, learning your lessons, eating your meals and being with friends, the little tortoise has been very busy indeed. Let me tell you what he has been up to.

First of all I expect you will remember that when our little tortoise left the store through the hole, it was raining outside and Saffron had pushed and shoved him up close to a pair of young dogs. Well, the puppies began to nudge him with their snouts. 'Who are you?' barked one. 'WHAT are you?' barked the other. They touched the tortoise with their muddy paws and gently batted him from one to the other – they were being careful with him but they were very curious to know what their mother had brought for them to play with.

Now maybe you think that the little tortoise would be scared by this attention from the puppies but, as a matter of fact, he was enjoying the feeling of moving along the earth, sliding in the wet mud. He liked the smell of the rain and the feel of the cool air against his head. And so he didn't disappear into his shell. Indeed he was enjoying everything so much that a strange sound bubbled up from inside him and out through his mouth. At first it was like a little mountain stream trickling over pebbles and then it got louder and louder. It sounded a little bit like the noise the plates had made when they were teasing him but it was a much more pleasant sound, a sound full of rainbow colours, a sound that made the little tortoise feel good all over.

'He's laughing,' exclaimed the chocolate brown puppy, collapsing into giggles herself and rolling over onto her back with her four paws waving in the air.

Her brother puppy gently nipped her ear and she giggled even more and wriggled in the mud like a sparrow taking a bath. Then she stood and shook a muddy spray of rain all over her mother. Saffron smiled but felt that she needed to remind her pups of their manners.

'Children, children. Calm down now! This little tortoise needs our help and we must be kind to him.'

The giggly puppy composed herself and put on a pretend serious face. She made a puppy curtsey to the little tortoise and said solemnly, 'How do you do. My name is Coco. May I ask what your name is?'

The little tortoise hesitated for a moment then said, 'Excuse me but I don't have a name yet.'

Coco put her head on one side and looked thoughtful. 'That's a shame,' she said. 'I hope that you find your name soon.'

The little tortoise was puzzled. 'Did you *find* your name somewhere? I thought the man would give me a name but he never did.'

Here Saffron spoke up again. 'Your given name and your found name are sometimes different, little one. We all found our names at the grocer's store where we live. This, by the way, is Pepper.'

Pepper, who was black with white paws and white ears and a large white patch around one eye, made a puppy bow and then sneezed all over the little tortoise who politely ignored this unfortunate accident.

Names are very important aren't they? *If you could find your own name for special occasions – and it could be anything at all, perhaps even a name that has never been used before – what name would you like to have?*

Now – where were we? Oh yes! The little tortoise and the puppies had just introduced themselves when they heard a cat hissing loudly. Spanner (who found her name in the bicycle repair shop) had just emerged from the old man's store and her white coat was already plastered with mud.

'I'm wet and cold from my nose to my tail,' she complained. 'This is no time to be standing around making polite conversation.'

Saffron raised one eyebrow and said quietly to the little tortoise 'Cats hate getting wet – we'd better get going and find you a dry place to sleep for the night.' Then she barked some instructions to her pups. 'Coco – you take front look-out position; Pepper – rear guard'. She began to nose the little tortoise into position. 'Lead on Spanner, we're ready now.'

Spanner shook her wet fur and shivered despite her best efforts not to. 'No self-respecting cat would deliberately go out in the rain,' she wailed irritably. 'I must be mad!'

The small convoy set off in the direction of the bicycle repair shop with Saffron pushing the little tortoise through the wet mud. It seemed like a very long journey. The little tortoise started off with his head sticking out because he wanted to see as much as he could of where he was going. But he kept getting mud in his eyes and he had to wait until Saffron pushed him through a puddle to clean his face again. Then Saffron said that it made it harder for her to push him if he kept looking around him all the time. So eventually he drew his head right into his shell and just tried to concentrate really hard on what he could hear and smell and feel. This is what he heard on the way to the bicycle repair store:

- the sound of the rain splashing on his shell and drumming on the metal roofs

- soft thudding sounds as Spanner leaped on and off walls to try to avoid putting her paws in the mud

- the slow steady sound of Saffron's breathing as she pushed him along as carefully as she could

- the splutter of Pepper sneezing

- the high pitched buzz of energetic mosquitoes

- a cricket rasping angrily because it had been woken up by the convoy.

These were all the things that the little tortoise heard as he travelled. *What do you think he touched as he travelled? What do you think he could smell? What feelings do you think he was having as he travelled? If you were setting off on an adventure like this, what would you be feeling inside?*

Then the little tortoise heard slip-slap, slip-slap. It was Malakaw, the mynah bird from the Council, slapping his yellow feet in the mud next to him. He was muttering to himself so quietly that the rest of the convoy had no chance of making out what he was saying.

'I should be asleep…fool's errand this…all for the sake of a bit of tin…who would have thought it… Ah…then again…maybe…yes… My, but you're a clever one to think of this…no one to see…pups out on patrol… Is it me or do they start training these patrol dogs at a younger age these days?' And on and on he muttered, slip-slapping his awkward way through the mud.

After what seemed like a very long time the little tortoise heard a clunk and realised that it was his own shell banging against something hard.

'Oops,' said Coco who had temporarily taken over the task of pushing the little tortoise to his destiny. 'Looks like we're stopping here for the rest of the night.'

She reached across with one paw and slid her new friend backwards, away from the offending obstacle. The little tortoise peeked out from his shell once more and saw that he was now very near to a huge door made of metal. In the dark he could just make out that it was red and somewhat rusty and that it stretched upwards and outwards further than he could see from so close up. Spanner was shaking her fur and arching her back against the rain.

'For goodness sake,' she hissed, 'Saffron – get us inside before my whiskers freeze and my tail shrinks.'

Saffron politely stopped herself from making a comment about how all of them were wet and tired and doing their very best. Instead she began snuffling around the base of the big metal door until she found the dog-sized hollow in the earth which she and her pups used for getting in and out of this disused store. She stretched out her front legs and wriggled her way through, pressing her stomach against the ground and practically flattening herself so that she would fit through the narrow space. Pepper followed close behind, accidentally kicking mud behind him as he went, much to the fury of Spanner who was close on his tail, anxious to get into the dry! Spanner hissed again and Pepper sneezed to cover his giggles. Then Coco pushed the little tortoise through the hole and squeezed through herself.

Malakaw watched the proceedings but chose not to follow the others – the inside of a deserted store was no place for a mynah bird that night – he had an important mission of his own.

Spanner soon found herself a dry spot where she could sit and clean her wet fur. Saffron and the pups, exhausted by this journey at the end of an already long day were settling themselves in another corner of the store, turning round and round to find the most comfortable position on the lumpy earthen floor. They had nudged the little tortoise into the middle of their group so that they could keep an eye on him. He too was very sleepy. He had discovered so many new sensations since leaving the old man's store and he had made his first big decision in life – a decision based on the Council's recommendation admittedly, but none the less a decision that he felt proud of.

As he began to drift off into sleep he was aware that Saffron was gently licking the mud from his shell in between cleaning the fur of her sleeping pups. Coco's front legs were twitching slightly – perhaps she was already dreaming about chasing a mongoose!

Outside the deserted store Malakaw had made his departure, flying quietly into the dark night sky and looking very much like a bat out hunting for food.

Expansion topics

- Talk about what makes a good friend. **Activity sheet 16**.

- What do you like to be called? Talk about your name and about how you got your name.

- Talk about feeling good about being yourself. Talk about praise. **Activity sheet 17**.

- Talk about all the different senses that we use.

5

Coping with Worries

Hello again. Are you ready to hear the next part of the story? Well, let me tell you that while you have been away the little tortoise has been worrying about lots of different things. *Can you think what his worries were?*

Up until now he had kept all these worries to himself because he hadn't had the chance to tell anyone. To be honest, he wasn't sure if anyone would want to hear them. Saffron and the pups had been very kind but there had certainly not been a chance to talk to them during the journey or once they had safely arrived at the empty store. Some of his worries had been about the pans and pots and plates and he hadn't wanted to tell these to the saucepan. He wasn't sure if Spanner would be interested or helpful and Malakaw had disappeared. So when he fell asleep he was still carrying all his worries around with him and this made his shell feel very heavy on his back. *What would you do if you were the little tortoise? Would you tell anyone about your worries?*

It was soon morning and Saffron was the first to wake. The puppies were still dozing when she gently nudged the little tortoise and called to him to come out from his shell. He emerged rather sleepily and peered at her through half closed eyes.

'Spanner and Malakaw are going to take you the rest of the way to the bicycle repair shop now, small one,' she said quietly. 'It's not a long journey but I'm afraid the pups and I must leave you for now. We have to travel to Flic-en-Flac – it's Thursday and we must be there to keep a watch on the schoolchildren at the beach and make sure they stay safe while they have their lunch'. She looked at the little tortoise for a moment or two in silence. 'We will come and look for you again soon, small one, but take heed of the saucepan's words – go wisely and beware of false friends.'

Coco began to stir from her dreams and Pepper sneezed a half-asleep sort of sneeze. The little tortoise wasn't at all sure what Saffron meant by 'false friends' but he promised to take care, and when the pups were fully awake and ready for their day, he thanked everyone for their help and said that he hoped he would see them again soon.

The pups were eager to set off for the beach as it was quite a long journey and they needed to find their breakfast on the way, but they each said a special goodbye and wished the little tortoise lots of luck.

He watched them squeeze through the hollow under the door of the store and sighed quietly to himself. It was hard to see his friends leave and not know when he would see them again. *Have you ever had that feeling?*

So, in the disused store, the little tortoise suddenly realised that he was all alone. Spanner was nowhere to be seen and everything was strangely quiet. He thought that maybe Spanner had simply gone outside to find herself some breakfast so he waited patiently for her to return.

To help the time pass he decided to try and practise rolling onto his side as he had seen the plates do in the old man's store when they rolled past the big saucepan to be inspected.

First he tried to shuffle along the floor. He could make himself move just a little bit if he really concentrated, but it was extremely difficult for him and he felt as if he was scratching the smooth tin of the underneath part of his body.

So then he tried rocking from side to side. This seemed to take even more effort, but was more successful. By moving his whole body inside his shell he could tip himself just slightly off the floor – first one side, then the other – left, then right; left, then right. He began to feel a little bit sick and very bruised but he was quite determined to master it. Left, then right, left, then right, left, then…oh! He had tried so hard and for so long that he had suddenly flipped himself right over and now he was upside down!

It took a while for him to catch his breath. 'Be brave,' he said to himself. 'You can work this one out.' Just for the moment though he was too exhausted to try and flip himself back again. He lay looking up at the ceiling of the store. He could see that there was a large hole at one end of the roof. It was still raining a little bit, but the sun was shining as well and the morning light was now flooding the building.

Through the hole, the little tortoise could see an arch of colours stretching across a patch of blue. He counted seven colours in the arch and he thought how beautiful it looked – like a magic bridge high up above him. And then as he watched, some soft white clouds drifted across the hole in the roof and the rainbow melted back into the sky.

He would have stayed on his back a little while longer, but he thought that he'd better try and turn himself the right way up before Spanner returned, and he guessed that this might take him some time. He was right. He twisted and rocked on the lumpy earthen floor for at least five minutes before with one last supreme effort he found he'd built up enough of a movement to flip himself right over. The view was not so interesting this way up but he certainly felt less dizzy!

With all this moving around the little tortoise found that he was now facing the hollow under the door and he waited patiently for the first signs of Spanner returning. He waited…and he waited…and he waited…but there was no sign of the white cat. Suddenly the silence of the store was broken by a clattering sound on the roof top and then a familiar face appeared through the hole that led out to the sky.

'Well, good mooorning,' crooned Malakaw. 'And how are we this morning?'

'Fine, thank you,' replied the little tortoise politely, 'And how are you?'

'Fine. Fine,' said Malakaw. 'Although my left leg has a bit of an ache in it and my beak is slightly chipped. Come to think of it, I lost a wing feather last night as well.'

The little tortoise was unsure how to respond to this list of problems, but tried to look sympathetic. Malakaw shuffled around the hole, rocking un-steadily on his yellow feet as he peered further into the store. He was checking that Saffron and the pups had left and that no one else had come to see the little tortoise.

All he could hear was the faint chattering of a gecko coming from somewhere in the shadows, but he was satisfied that such a tiny creature posed no threat to him.

He dipped his head and flew down onto the floor. He was trailing a long piece of woven straw from his yellow beak.

'I've come to let you know that Spanner is unwell – a cold in the head from being out in the rain for so long last night, she says. So I'm going to take you to the bicycle repair shop and she will join us later when she's fully recovered.'

He started to do a little dance around the tortoise who soon realised that Malakaw was tying the piece of straw right round his tin shell. It was done in a flash and tied in a sort of a knot, as best as a bird can manage, under the little tortoise's chin.

'Now – here we go,' said Malakaw. He hopped awkwardly across the floor of the store with the other end of the straw held firmly in his beak. The tortoise found himself dragged along the bumpy floor and then, as Malakaw squawked and squirmed his way under the door, he was suddenly pulled out into the open air again.

Another, bigger mynah bird stood waiting for them outside. He had ap-parently been keeping watch to make sure no-one noticed what was happening. He ignored the little tortoise and spoke sharply to Malakaw who was trying to shake the dirt from his ruffled feathers.

'Be quick…no time to lose…must be there before the main delivery.'

Malakaw coughed and nodded as he couldn't say anything at all just at that moment. He took up the straw binding in his beak again and began to drag the little tortoise along the path, just a few hops at a time. The streets were almost empty as it was so early in the morning, but progress was slow and the two birds had to keep taking turns at hauling their load.

The little tortoise had no idea how long it would take to get to the bicycle repair shop. He wished that Saffron and her pups were still with him – Malakaw and his friend were not being very talkative and the little tortoise missed the friendliness of the pups and their mother. On and on they travelled. Sometimes they would stop unexpectedly if anyone walked too close. Then the two birds would flutter inelegantly around the tortoise or even sit on top of him to hide him from prying eyes!

The journey seemed to take for ever but at last, just when the little tortoise thought that he couldn't make it any further, Malakaw collapsed in a little heap and spluttered, 'Here we are then.'

But, oh, what a shock for the poor tortoise! When he looked around him he quickly realised that this was not the bicycle repair shop at all – it was a *recycling* centre! Before he had time to disappear into his shell he heard heavy footsteps and right in front of his nose appeared two large leather boots with two big legs stretching up from them. The man was standing so close to the little tortoise that this was all he could see of him. He heard another man speak.

'Well, what have those crazy birds brought us today, Vikram?'

Vikram leant over and lifted the straw binding so that the little tortoise was dangling in mid air. 'No idea! What do you think this is then?' he said. 'A fancy bowl? A doorstop? Can't make it out!'

'Well, maybe we'll melt it down and use it for something later – give the birds those fish heads and get rid of them.'

Vikram dropped the little tortoise on to the ground again and delved into a bucket for the fish heads to feed the offending birds. They ate greedily – it had been hard work dragging the little tortoise all this way – and while they ate they carefully avoided making eye contact with the now upside down tortoise.

What a terrible thing to happen – to be tricked in this way by a couple of mynah birds! Poor little tortoise felt very confused. Perhaps these birds were the false friends that the saucepan and Saffron had talked about.

And what of Spanner? She had left him alone in the empty store – was she a false friend too? While the little tortoise was trying to collect his thoughts he felt himself being picked up again. Vikram was examining him very closely, turning him over and over.

'Maybe not for melting down – maybe I'll just put it in the shed 'til I figure out what to do with it. Looks a bit special – better than the usual stuff those birds bring us.'

And that's how the little tortoise found himself in the shed where Vikram kept special things that he didn't want to recycle. Vikram even gave him a polish with an old piece of cloth dipped in rain water before placing him safely in a corner on top of a pile of old books. This was turning out to be a huge adventure, thought the little tortoise, wondering what on earth could possibly happen next.

Outside the shed, Vikram was sharing his lunch with a black and white puppy who had just appeared. He stroked the puppy and tugged its ears gently, and the puppy sneezed.

Expansion topics

- Talk about talking. Who can you talk to about things that worry you?

- Make a group/class list of times when it's easy to talk to people and times when it's harder to talk to people. **Activity sheet 18**.

- Talk about what can be done with worries. **Activity sheets 19–21**.

- How do you think the little tortoise felt when Saffron and the pups had to go away to do other things?

- Talk about making mistakes and trying again. How is this useful?

- Talk about times when being a friend is difficult. Talk about 'false' friends. **Activity sheet 22**.

- What might the old man have felt if he realised that the tortoise was missing from his store?

6

Choices

Welcome back again. I wonder if you can remember where the little tortoise was when we last visited the story? Who did he meet at the recycling centre? What was the last thing that happened? Do you think the little tortoise had any choices about what to do next?

Well, in fact, there were *lots* of choices for him to make. Now that he was left alone in the shed he realised that he was feeling much more confident about what he could do. He knew that he could make himself move, even though this took a lot of effort. He knew that he could cope with being pulled and pushed through mud and shoved through holes without getting dented and scratched too much. This made him feel more able to face new things, even when something unexpected happened. He knew that he could make decisions. And he knew that others would actually listen to what he had to say, and take his thoughts and feelings seriously. He was beginning to understand his feelings more easily as well (although he wished that he didn't have quite so many different ones to cope with!).

So now the little tortoise could choose to feel scared and miserable or he could choose to be brave; he could choose to think that everyone had abandoned him or he could choose to remember that he had made some new friends and that they would be worried about him when he didn't turn up at the bicycle repair shop. He could stay on top of this pile of books and do nothing at all and just see what happened or he could try and get down and have a look around. *What choices would you make if you were the little tortoise? Think of some good choices and some that would not be so good.*

Well, with his new-found confidence and feeling really quite brave the little tortoise chose to try and get off the pile of books. He rocked himself from side to side in the way that he had practised the day before, until he rocked himself right off the books and onto the floor with a clatter. Outside, Vikram heard the noise and looked up from playing with the puppy, 'Those nosy birds – bet they've got into the shed again.'

He stood up and marched towards the shed with Pepper following close on his heels. When he opened the door Pepper darted between his legs, spotted the little tortoise and bounded towards him in a flash.

'Pepper! Thank goodness!' whispered the little tortoise. And before he knew what was happening Pepper had the woven straw between his teeth and was pulling him out of the shed.

'Whoa, little fella!' cried Vikram, bending down and grabbing Pepper by the scruff of his neck. 'Where are you going with that?'

Pepper wagged his tail and kept hold of the tortoise as if to say, 'I'm just playing.' Vikram laughed.

'That's too good a toy for a dog, I think – and it's not very easy to drag with no wheels on!'

'Wheels?' thought the little tortoise. He was sure that wheels were big round things that bikes had. How could *he* possibly have wheels? Pepper had seen wheels too. He had seen bicycle wheels and he had seen wheels on toys as well. His patrol training meant that he had already spotted a box full of wheels of all different sizes in the shed. Now he dropped the woven straw, wriggled free from Vikram's grasp and bounded over to the box, jumping onto it and wagging his tail again.

'Well, well' said Vikram, 'it's almost as if you knew what I'd said!'

He strode over to Pepper and lifted him onto the floor then tipped out the contents of the box.

'Now, let's see…blue ones…no…yellow…too rusty…how about these then?' He held up four small wheels that looked like they'd once been part of a remote controlled car. 'We could use these, no problem at all. What do you think, pup?'

Pepper danced his best dance around Vikram's feet and winked at the little tortoise.

'OK,' said Vikram, 'I'll soon have these fixed on.'

And he did just exactly that. He fixed the four wheels on to the ends of two little metal rods then he fixed the metal rods under the little tortoise's body, and it was all done in the twenty minutes when Vikram should have been finishing off his lunch! Then he put the tortoise on the floor and pulled on the woven straw to see if the wheels would work. They squeaked loudly and the little tortoise shot forward. The sudden movement caught him completely by surprise! Part of him wanted to shout 'STOP!' and another part of him wanted to yell 'Hooray!' Perhaps you can remember when you first learnt to ride a bike or use roller skates. Perhaps it was a bit scary to suddenly be moving so fast on wheels, but perhaps it was also a bit exciting.

And then it was time for Vikram to get on with his work again. Pepper very cleverly danced around his feet and distracted him so that he left the shed door unlocked and slightly open because he was so busy ruffling Pepper's fur and throwing pebbles for him to catch.

The little tortoise was left alone in the shed to think about what had just happened. He had wheels! Not legs, like he'd expected, but small round shiny wheels with little plastic tyres on them to make them roll smoothly. *Can you imagine how he was feeling? See if you can think of some words to describe how the little tortoise might have felt about getting these wheels.*

When Vikram was a good distance away from the shed, busy sorting scrap metal into piles, Pepper felt that it was safe to return and fetch the little tortoise. He nuzzled at the shed door and pushed it open wide enough to squeeze through.

'Come on,' he panted, 'No time to lose.'

The little tortoise was still excited and wanted to thank Pepper and explain what it was like to have these amazing wheels – just exactly the right size for him and so shiny and smart and light and fitting so neatly onto the shiny metal rods and... But Pepper hushed the tortoise and picked up the woven straw between his teeth. He was in 'patrol leader' mode and knew that they had to move quickly and quietly to avoid being caught.

He peered outside to check that the coast was clear and then began to back out of the door, tail first so that he could keep an eye on how his friend was coping with being on wheels. The little tortoise began to glide along the floor again – easily and smoothly. *So* easily, in fact, that when Pepper paused to get a better grip on the straw, the wheels continued to turn and the little tortoise bumped right into Pepper's nose.

'OUCH!' yelled the puppy and then sneezed.

They both froze, certain that Vikram would have heard. They waited and listened and in that moment it seemed like every single thing in the shed, and indeed the shed itself, was holding its breath. The little tortoise lost the feeling of excitement and began to feel afraid. But, no, there were no other sounds – no signs of anyone outside having heard anything unusual. Pepper widened his eyes as if to say THAT was close! Then he picked up the straw again and tugged the little tortoise out into the open.

This was going to prove a real challenge. He was in charge of a major escape – not a beach watch, nor a stroll though the casuarina trees. He kept his ears pricked, listening intently. His nose twitched as he tried to note changes in the air and his eyes scanned this way and that. All his senses were primed, his whole body prepared for swift action if needed. Puppy patrol lessons were really paying off now and he felt more than ready for whatever dangers lay ahead.

Slowly, stealthily, they edged their way through the large yard of the recycling centre, both of them acutely aware of every squeak of the little tortoise's wheels and every clink of his shell against rocks and pieces of scrap that they had to negotiate their way past.

They had almost made it to the yard gates – almost made it to safety when Pepper heard the unmistakable sound of a truck coming towards them and Vikram's cry of 'delivreeee!' followed by the sound of approaching footsteps. Pepper had to think fast – no good trying to make a run for it – that would simply draw attention to them both. So he barked 'hide!'

As the little tortoise withdrew into his shell (because of course that's how a tortoise hides) Pepper flung himself on top of his friend in army commando style and lay there trying to look as though he was just taking a rest in the sun. The little tortoise could feel the fast beating of Pepper's heart even through his shell. Vikram came close to them. For one terrible, body trembling moment it seemed that he was going to try to chase Pepper away, but instead he bent down and scratched behind one of the puppy's ears.

'You still here then?' he asked, rather obviously.

Pepper wagged the end of his tail slightly and half closed his eyes as if enjoying the attention, but really wishing with all his might that Vikram would move on. Luckily, just then the driver of the truck shouted a greeting and drove the huge dusty vehicle further into the yard. He climbed from the cab, nodded to Vikram and let down the tail-board. To his horror, Pepper watched as Vikram walked around behind the truck and closed the enormous yard gates which had been left open for most of the day to allow people to come and go freely.

Now their planned escape route was well and truly blocked. Pepper scrutinised the fence on either side of the gates – it was close-woven wire fencing staked into the ground at about two metre intervals. It appeared well-maintained. There were no visible holes at ground level and Pepper calculated that it would leave the tortoise exposed for too long if he tried to dig an exit hollow under any part of the fence close by. The afternoon sun was beating down on his back and he desperately wanted to move himself and his friend into the shade, but the men were too close. They were walking to and from the back of the truck unloading old furniture, rusty sheets of corrugated metal and several big hessian sacks full of something that seemed to make them very heavy. Vikram and the truck driver grunted and pulled faces and took for ever to empty the truck and distribute the contents in various places around the yard. But finally it was done.

'Want a drink?' asked Vikram, wiping the sweat from his forehead.

'Yeh' replied the driver. 'Thought you'd never ask.'

He threw the now empty sacks into the back of the truck and followed Vikram towards the shed for a drink of papaya juice. Pepper waited until they were safely out of sight then took up the woven straw firmly between his teeth and winked at the little tortoise. He had a new plan. His heart was thumping with anticipation. He knew exactly what he had to do to save his friend. *Can you guess his plan? What plan would you have? Try and think of as many ways as possible that Pepper might solve this problem.*

And now, because this story wants us to help it out, we are going to make up our own ending to this part. We will finish with the words 'and that is how the little tortoise and Pepper escaped from the recycling centre and found their way back to the road outside Bambous Primary School'.

Expansion topics

- How do you think the little tortoise and Pepper were feeling? Do you think they were feeling the *same* feelings as each other or different feelings? Why do you think they were feeling these things? Did they have a choice about how they were feeling?

- How do you solve problems? **Activity sheets 23 and 24**.

- Think of a time when you have made a choice about what to do or where to go and you felt that you had made the right choice. How many different situations can you think of where you have a choice about things? Are there any situations you can think of when you don't have a choice?

- Talk about why physical achievements help us to feel good about ourselves. **Activity sheet 25**.

- As a group, or in pairs, make up the ending to this part of the story.

7

Different Perspectives

And so my friends, how did the last part of this story want to be finished? Ah yes, you remember we said 'and that is how the little tortoise and Pepper escaped from the recycling centre and found their way back to the road outside Bambous Primary School'.

So there they were. It was late in the afternoon and Pepper had pulled the little tortoise into a shady spot beneath a large tree just outside the school entrance. He knew that this time of the day was always busy and noisy as the children left school to go home. He guessed that no one would even notice a dog lying in the shade or, if they did, they would think it unremarkable. He didn't lie across the tortoise this time but placed his friend close up to the tree and then lay in front of him. In the dancing shadows around the base of the tree you could really hardly notice that he was there at all.

Pepper had whispered that they were to wait here until Saffron and Coco returned from Flic-en-Flac. They would be safer travelling together and they would wait until half past six when darkness had fallen and the streets would be quieter.

Pepper was getting very hungry again – the meagre lunch of samoussa and dal purri that he had shared with Vikram had not satisfied his need for food for very long, but he dared not leave the tortoise unprotected. So he tried to doze a little and he dreamt of eating left-over steak from a local res-taurant.

The little tortoise didn't know about the sensation of hunger because tin tortoises don't have to eat. He could hear Pepper's stomach rumbling and he wondered if his puppy friend was feeling alright. When he dozed, instead of dreaming of eating steak, he dreamt that he was 'free-wheeling' down a long, empty path, whooshing past buildings and trees and feeling the cool air flow over his head and shell, giving him a wonderful sense of freedom and enjoyment.

Time passed. Maybe a few seconds, maybe several minutes. The little tortoise woke suddenly. Even in his dreaming state he had sensed that someone was near. He peered over the top of Pepper's sleeping form. A little girl was crouching a short distance from him, watching him closely. Her black plaited hair fell loosely across one shoulder. There were no other children near by, only two women standing on the white verandah at the front of the school, talking intently. Neither of them were looking in his direction.

Pepper, too, had sensed that something was going on. He sneezed and opened his eyes. He looked at the little girl but did not make a move. He didn't want to encourage her to come closer. He thought about growling at her, but that might have frightened her and would draw the attention of the two women. So they just kept eye contact – the little girl and the puppy – sizing each other up, checking each other out. Eventually the little girl stood up and moved one step closer.

'I didn't know that you had wheels,' she said.

Pepper's heart sank. She had spotted the tortoise despite his best efforts. Then he felt a very slight touch against his body. The little tortoise was pressing his head against Pepper's side because of course he knew this little girl. Do you remember where they had met before? Yes, that's right, she had visited the old man's store and had said 'hello' to the little tortoise. He pushed harder against Pepper who finally got the message and moved away, though rather reluctantly.

'I think this puppy has taken you to play with and the man in the store will be worried when he sees you've gone.' She paused. 'I think,' she said very decisively, 'I should take you back to the store.' And she reached down and scooped up the little tortoise as quick as a flash and headed towards the two women.

Her mother turned and smiled.

'What have you got there dear? Does this belong to the school Miss Panchal?'

The teacher looked at the shiny object. 'No. One of the children must have left it by mistake. I wonder what it is. Where did you find it Lovena?'

'Over by the tree, Miss. It's a tortoise and I know where it comes from. It's from the store that Daddy took me to yesterday. Can we take it back there, Mummy?'

'Well, I think we should,' said Lovena's mother. She looked at her watch. 'We can do it on the way home if you're sure that's where it comes from.'

'Oh, for sure I'm sure, and…well…if it's for sale, could I have it, do you think? Could I, please?'

Lovena's mother smiled again and exchanged a knowing look with Miss Panchal – one of those special looks that grown-ups use when they think they are sharing a piece of knowledge about children that the children themselves are not supposed to know. *Lovena* knew though, and she crossed her fingers and wished as hard as she could. The little tortoise looked down from his perch in Lovena's arms and tried to smile reassuringly at Pepper who was still standing very close.

Poor Pepper. He felt that he had failed in his mission. He had helped his friend to escape from the recycling centre only to see him returned to the store that the Council had been so definite that he should leave. He was determined to make sure that his friend stayed safe, and so he decided he would follow the little girl and her mother to the store and see what happened.

And what about Spanner – do you remember her? The white cat who left the little tortoise all alone in the deserted store when she was supposed to be looking after him. Well, if we look at the story from a slightly different angle – from above maybe, or from the left or the right instead of straight on, then we will see Spanner asleep in her cat basket. She is curled up in a fluffy ball, her fur looking slightly more dull than usual. If her eyes were open you would see that they were a bit red, and when she breathes she sounds as though she is wheezing. Last night Lovena gave her some cat medicine and it does seem to be helping a bit. She also made sure that Spanner (known to her as 'pusskins') couldn't get out of the house as she was worried that she had cat flu.

You see, Spanner had slipped out of the empty store in the early morning because she was suspicious of Malakaw. Not wanting to alarm the others about a potential traitor in the Council she had gone to seek advice from the saucepan, but on the way she had suddenly felt very ill and had needed to rest for a while. She thought she might just go home and have the breakfast that she knew Lovena would have put out for her. And that, of course, is where she ended up staying for the rest of the day because she was so poorly.

But Spanner was resourceful and she had sent a messenger gecko to the empty store to see that the tortoise was alright and to report back to Coco and the pups when they returned from Flic-en-Flac. That is how Pepper had been able to find his friend at the recycling centre.

When you heard the first part of this story perhaps you thought that Spanner was a villain and had plotted with Malakaw to get rid of the little tortoise. Sometimes we make things up in our heads that seem so true to us that we believe they really *are* true. Then we don't bother to check the facts.

We just go through the day making decisions and doing things and thinking things based on this belief that isn't real at all! *Can you think of a time when that has happened to you?* Sometimes we just don't know the real story until we look closer or ask the right questions and listen carefully to each other.

So we will thank our story for showing us the truth about Spanner and we will return now to the old man's store to see what has been happening there. *What questions should we ask the story now? What would you like to know so that we can discover the fate of the little tortoise?*

Lovena and her mother went to see the old man on the way home from Lovena's school. He was concentrating hard, his head bent low over his work. When he looked up and saw Lovena holding the little tortoise he had a whole mixture of feelings all at once. *What do you think he felt?*

Well the story tells us that the old man felt surprised because he hadn't even realised that the tortoise had gone. He had been determined not to look on the shelf today or be distracted by thoughts of his grandchild. He felt delight too. Delight at seeing Lovena with her mother. He liked it when children came to the store with their parents – they brought a bit of sparkle and laughter to his tired old heart. He felt pride at seeing the shiny tortoise carried so carefully and lovingly by this little girl. And, yes, he still felt sadness for his own family. Then he noticed that the tortoise had wheels and a strand of woven straw around it, so that it could be pulled along. And he was puzzled at that, but he smiled because the little tortoise looked 'completed'.

Lovena laid the tortoise on the workbench and looked hopefully at her mother.

'Good afternoon,' her mother said.

'Good afternoon,' responded the old man, 'And good afternoon to you little girl. I see you have found my tortoise and that it has somehow got itself some wheels. I'm very grateful to you for returning it.'

'Ah!' said Lovena's mother and then seemed unsure how to proceed.

'We were wondering,' chirruped her daughter, flicking her plait over her shoulder, 'We were wondering, if you hadn't already sold the tortoise to someone else, and if you did then they must have been very careless because they left it at the school and may be they shouldn't have had it in the first place and…'

'We were wondering,' said her mother, 'If you would sell us the tortoise.'

The old man was amazed. He looked from the tortoise to Lovena and back to the tortoise again. He was sure that he could see the tortoise smiling. But, no, that must have been his imagination. Behind his head the plates were having a hard time sitting still on the shelf and as for the big saucepan well –

it was very close to blowing its cover! They were willing the man to say 'Yes'. They were so excited for the little tortoise.

And, of course, after thinking about it for only a short while he did say 'Yes'. Then the old man and Lovena's mother arranged a suitable price, and money exchanged hands. Everyone seemed very pleased with the whole transaction (especially the little tortoise).

'You know,' said Lovena's mother, 'The carvings on this shell are wonderful. Would you be able to make another tortoise like this for my nephew?'

The old man remembered that while he had been making the tortoise he had really enjoyed doing something so different for a change and he thought yes, may be he *could* make another tortoise and he would give it wheels and he would work out a way that the woven straw could be attached to it so that it could be pulled along easily. They were still discussing this when Lovena noticed that the little black and white dog had followed them all the way from the school and was sitting under the old man's workbench.

'Your dog is so clever,' she said to the old man. 'He was looking after the little tortoise all the time.'

'But I don't have a dog,' replied the old man. He followed Lovena's gaze to beneath the workbench and saw Pepper sitting there, wagging his tail.

'Well, well,' he mused, 'I've seen this puppy before – he's usually with two other dogs and I know they live behind the grocery store.'

Even though the old man had always said that he didn't really like dogs very much, he found himself bending down and stroking Pepper behind the ears.

'You look like you've made yourself quite at home there, young pup. I wonder if I can find you some food, seeing as you took such good care of the tortoise for us.'

Pepper licked the old man's hand and then made a doggy bow to the little tortoise. To everyone else it just looked as though he was having a bit of a stretch, but the tortoise knew that it was his way of saying goodbye to him. He felt very lucky to have made such a special friend.

Pepper felt lucky too. He had a new friend and he'd had an exciting adventure that had tested his puppy patrol skills. He thought that may be he had also found a new home since he was really old enough to leave his first home now. He decided to check this out with Saffron and Coco that very night.

And Lovena carefully carried the little tortoise all the way to *his* new home (although he would have much preferred to have used his wheels). When they got there she placed him gently on the floor and her mother gave her a small oil can so that she could oil the wheels. Now when the little tortoise moved, he didn't squeak! He thought that he could never be happier than he was at that moment as he started to move around the kitchen floor and Lovena had him doing circles and half turns and going fast and going slow and gliding, oh so effortlessly, across the cool tiles.

Then, as he slid past the kitchen table, he spotted Spanner blinking at him from her cat basket. He saw that she was not well and he knew instantly, the way that only a tin tortoise with wheels can know, that Spanner was his friend and not his enemy and that they would be the very best of friends! There was just one more thing that the little tortoise wished for. *Can you imagine what that might have been? Can you remember what it was that the Council said he should set off to find when he left the old man's store?* Yes, you're right of course, he hadn't found his name yet. But now Spanner crept from her basket and came over to greet the tortoise and to see if all was well. She peered at his wheels and coughed.

'Well,' she said, blinking, 'You've been carrying your name around with you all this time!'

And indeed he had! Printed clearly on all four tyres were the words 'Built for endurance and reliability' followed by a name. *What do you think that name was? Choose a special name, one that you think would be just right! Imagine yourself whispering the name to the little tortoise. What does he do when he hears it? It's a wonderful name for a little tortoise don't you think?*

And that, my friends, is how the little tortoise found out who he was.

Now, before we leave this story, it has just one more thing to tell us. You see, just like one of the pieces of a patchwork quilt, the story of the little tin tortoise in Mauritius attaches to the edges of other stories and they, in turn, attach to more stories. So, even though the tin tortoise is very small, his adventures form a most important part of the patchwork of stories.

If we look closely we will see that his adventures are connected to a story about the old man's family and that this connection happens because one day – and maybe you had already guessed this – the old man made a tortoise for his grandson and he wrote a long letter and he put the tortoise and the letter in a parcel and posted it to the last address he had for his son in England. This new tortoise had a wonderful adventure all of its own…but that's a whole new story!

Well then, here we are. With your help and my help this particular story has arrived at its ending and, very wonderfully, we have arrived with it! As it draws to a close, everything folds away so we can tuck it into our minds. Some of you might carry one bit of the story around for a while, some of you might carry a different bit. Perhaps sometimes you will feel as though you are in the story because something will remind you of a feeling or a thought that the little tortoise had. And that is the magic of this story you see – it happened a long time ago and yet it only happened yesterday and today…or maybe, just maybe…it will happen tomorrow!

Expansion topics

- Talk about different perspectives. How many can you find in the last part of this story?

- Talk about coping with unexpected things.

- Talk about times when you have felt brave enough or confident enough to do something that was a bit difficult for you. **Activity sheet 26**.

- How do you think the little tortoise felt when he found his name?

- Make a group list of all the things that you think the little tortoise learned during his adventures.

- Imagine that you are the old man. What would you write in your letter to your son?

- Talk about how the stories of each of our lives join with or touch the stories of other people's lives too. What we do affects other people around us and what other people do has an effect upon us.

- In groups or pairs make up a short story about what happened to the tortoise that was sent to England.

Part 3

Practical Resources

Appendix A

Activity Sheets
and Guidance Notes

1. How many feelings?
– Storyteller notes

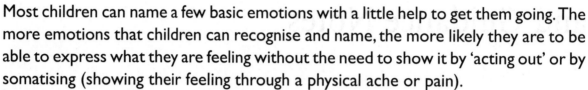

Most children can name a few basic emotions with a little help to get them going. The more emotions that children can recognise and name, the more likely they are to be able to express what they are feeling without the need to show it by 'acting out' or by somatising (showing their feeling through a physical ache or pain).

It is important to help children to understand that all feelings are real and valid and that they have some choice in how they express their feelings. Anger doesn't have to lead to physical aggression; feeling scared or anxious doesn't have to lead to avoidance; feeling excited doesn't always have to involve running around the room like a wild horse!

Stand in a circle and do a round of 'I feel_____'. Encourage each child to take turns to jump into the circle and show the group how they are feeling today (by physical posture and facial expression). Ask the rest of the group to copy the non-verbal aspects of this feeling so that the child in the centre can see what this looks like. This exercise, especially if done regularly, encourages children to recognise their own feelings and those of others. It is also a great boost to self-esteem to have a feeling validated by watching others as they try to 'see how it feels'.

Of course, this works equally well with just one adult and one child.

I. How many feelings?

The little tortoise had many different feelings but he couldn't name them all. It is important to know about our feelings. They are part of who we are.

Here are a few different words that describe how we can feel.

Happy   Sad   Excited   Angry   Disappointed

Write down as many more feeling words as you can. Then collect some more words from your friends and family by asking them how they are feeling.

sad

happy   excited

angry   disappointed

2. How I feel – Storyteller notes

- Choose two situations from the completed activity sheets and discuss whether other children in the group (or you) have been in a similar situation but felt something different.

- Compare all the different things that lead to each child feeling excited or nervous.

- Talk about how different people feel different things at different times.

- Talk about how feelings can change – what we might once have been nervous about we might eventually come to enjoy or to feel confident about.

- Point out any feelings that are similar in the group ('It sounds as though most of you get excited when _____', 'Almost everyone feels nervous when _____. 'Both of us feel disappointed when _____.')

2. How I feel

Having a feeling doesn't mean that you are always going to be like that. The little tortoise felt lonely and confused but that doesn't mean that he is always going to be lonely or will always be confused.

Imagine some times when you have felt some of these feelings. Draw or write about each of the feelings listed on this page.

A time when I felt very brave was…

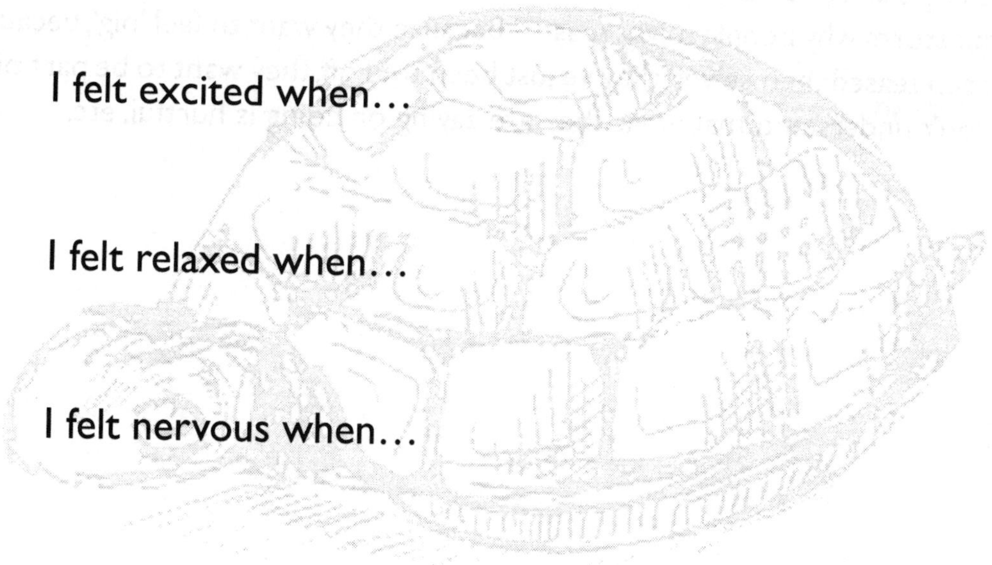

I felt excited when…

I felt relaxed when…

I felt nervous when…

I felt angry when…

I felt happy when…

I felt disappointed when…

3. Teasing and bullying
– Storyteller notes

Discussions about teasing can be lengthy. The intensity of focused concentration may need to be relieved by an active game at the end of this topic.

Persistent teasing is, of course, a type of bullying. Children with low self-esteem are invariably either the victim of teasing or bullying or resort to being the teaser/bully themselves.

Brainstorm different ways that people tease each other such as name-calling, taking and playing with treasured possessions, copying the way that someone walks or talks, consistently ignoring someone and so on.

Is there such a thing as 'OK teasing'? At what point does 'having fun' become something that is not OK?

Brainstorm why people might tease – because they want to feel 'big', because they have been teased themselves, they've just been told off, they want to be part of a gang, they don't understand that what they are saying or doing is hurtful, etc.

3. Teasing and bullying

Let's spend a little time thinking about something that is not a friendly thing to do. The plates were laughing at the little tortoise and this upset him. Have you ever been teased?

Have you ever teased someone else?

Is teasing the same as bullying?

Think of different ways that someone might tease another person.

Now think about *why* people might tease others.

How do you think it feels to tease someone else?

4. More on teasing
– Storyteller notes

When you brainstorm 'what to do' be sure to accept all the contributions, even if you do not agree with some of them. Once you have collected all the ideas, talk about the consequences of each action. What would happen if you hit the person? What would happen if you told a grown-up? Children have often been told to 'ignore' the person who is teasing, but I have never yet had a group where all the members agreed on this strategy. Many children tell me they've tried this 'but it doesn't work'. This might be because they need to come up with a *way* of ignoring. For example 'I can name thirty different fruits in my head so that I can't hear what the person is saying' or 'I can turn and walk away and think about something nice that is going to happen at the weekend'.

Brainstorming the options and their consequences usually results in some useful ideas that children are more likely to try because they have thought of these solutions themselves.

4. More on teasing

How does it feel to be teased? Think of as many words as you can that describe what people might feel like when they are teased.

Now let's think of some things that you could do.

If I was being teased I could…

If I saw someone else being teased I would…

I would not…

5. Everyone is different
– Storyteller notes

Think about 'sameness' in such things as looks, actions, likes and dislikes. Discuss similarities and differences in the answers that are given. Expand on some of the themes by asking questions such as 'Why would that be difficult?' 'And *then* what would happen?'

Invite children to come up with some fantastical answers to this as well as more logical ones!

5. Everyone is different

The little tin tortoise spent a long time wondering if he should pretend to be a bowl. Imagine what it would be like if each of us were exactly the same. Imagine what your family would be like.

What about your class or your street or your town or the world?!

What would be one good thing about everyone being the same?

What would *not* be good about all being the same?

How are you different from one of your friends?

6. Something in common?
– Storyteller notes

Talk about different areas of 'commonality'. For example, talk about the different groups that children might be members of – school groups, family groups, sports teams, etc. The aim is to help children to look beyond physical things that they might have in common to such things as leisure interests and common aims.

6. Something in common?

How was the little tortoise similar to some of the other things in the store?

Sometimes you can find ways that people are similar. For example, people can be alike in the way that they look, how they behave, where they live, what they like to do or to eat and what they *don't* like. Find someone in your class or group who is like you in some way.

What is their name?

How is this person like you?

Do you know someone who is like you in *lots* of ways? What is their name?

How are they like you?

This is called 'having something in common'.

7. Who am I? – Storyteller notes

Writing a 'character sketch' can help to promote greater awareness of self and others. It is based on an idea developed by personal construct psychologists/therapists.

Some children may find this exercise quite difficult, having little idea of how others might see them or how they see themselves. They may need some prompts in the form of questions such as 'what would your best friend say about the way that you _____'?

7. Who am I?

What has the little tortoise learnt about himself so far? For example, what does he like? What doesn't he like? Write a short description of the little tortoise as if you were describing him to someone who has not heard the story.

Now have a go at describing yourself. Imagine that you are your best friend talking about you. What would your friend say? For example, what might he or she say about what you like doing and what you are good at? What might they say about what you don't like doing and about what worries you? Begin with your name:

_____ is…

8. I would like to be...
– Storyteller notes

By comparing and contrasting themselves with someone else, children can explore differences and similarities and also begin to think about future possibilities. Is there anything about this other person that might be an appropriate goal to start to work towards or something to think about as a goal for the future?

8. I would like to be...

Imagine that you could be someone else for a day, perhaps someone famous or one of your friends or someone in your family. Who would you choose to be? Why would you choose to be this person?

As this person, think about your day. What would you do? How would you behave? What would you do well? What would you have to eat? How would your day be different or the same to a day in your real life? What would be the best thing about being this person? Is there anything that would be difficult?

9. Imagining that feelings are colours – Storyteller notes

Our moods change and that means that uncomfortable feelings, as well as nice feelings, will change, stop or fade away gradually.

Feelings could be explored as if they were different animals or sounds, etc. but for this activity the children are invited to think about feelings as if they were colours. Talk about how we can feel like a different colour at different times on different days.

Talk about how two people could feel like the same colour for completely different reasons.

Help the children to elaborate on how they would move if they were being different colours. Invite two or more children at a time to move around the room as if they were being a certain feeling 'colour'. See if the rest of the group can correctly guess the colour.

9. Imagining that feelings are colours

The little tortoise was learning about lots of new feelings. Sometimes you can use your imagination to help you to describe how you are feeling.

Perhaps if I were a colour instead of a person then I would be the colour red today because I feel very energetic. Maybe someone else would be the colour red because they feel very brave and strong. Yesterday I might have been the colour blue because I felt very calm.

Imagine that you are a colour. Which colour would you be today?

If I were a colour I would be…

Because…

Imagine yourself being this colour. How do you move as this colour? Do you make a sound? If so, what sound do you make? What do you feel like as this colour?

10. Growing happy feelings – Storyteller notes

Children can find it very hard to cope when their feelings change too frequently and too quickly. Brainstorm ideas for what we can do to keep our feelings more balanced. For example, if I keep getting angry I can:

- tell someone that I'm feeling angry

- sit and do a quiet activity until I feel more calm

- go and scribble in an 'angry book'

- write down all the things I'm angry about

- think about what I'm going to do later that I'm looking forward to

- daydream about the thing I'd like to happen that would mean I wasn't angry any more (wouldn't it be wonderful if I could have that new computer game/stay up late/go to the park – if I was invisible/a giant/an adult/I would _____!)

Of course, sometimes children don't know why they are feeling something. Acknowledging an unpleasant feeling can still help to dissipate it without the need to analyse it.

Talk about the different ideas that everyone comes up with for growing happy feelings. Celebrate the differences!

10. Growing happy feelings

Sometimes feelings can change very quickly, perhaps because of something that happens to us or something that we hear or see. For example, I might be feeling very relaxed and then suddenly feel angry about something. It is important to remember that this new feeling will change as well.

There are often some things that we can do to help ourselves to feel differently. Let's imagine that you can grow happy feelings just like you can grow a plant.

Plants usually need a lot of looking after to help them to be at their best. Different plants need different sorts of earth. Some like shade and some like lots of sun. Some will only grow where it is very watery and some like to be quite dry.

In the same way, different people would like different things to help them to grow happy feelings. Write about or draw the things that you need for your happy feelings to grow.

Now ask someone else what things help them to feel happy.

11. Body talk – Storyteller notes

Talk about how we can show the same feeling in lots of different ways. Ask the children how they show that they are excited, for example. Some children may be very active when they are excited, some may use an 'excited' gesture like clapping their hands, and some may just smile or laugh.

Discuss the idea that we could show different emotions in almost the same way (for example a child could cry because he's sad or because he's angry) and we have to look for other clues to help us to know what the feeling really might be. Act out different emotions and see if the children can guess the feeling. Talk about 'obvious' body language and more subtle actions like looking away.

11. Body talk

How did the little tortoise show how he was feeling? Did he show the same feeling in different ways? Did he show different feelings in the same way?

Sometimes it is possible to know how someone is feeling even before they say anything. They show us how they feel by the way they are standing or sitting or moving and by the expression on their face.

How do you think someone would look if they were angry? See if you can draw an angry person.

Let's imagine
Close your eyes and imagine someone you know. What does this person look like when they are happy? How do they stand? Do you think they would be moving their hands or would they be still? What does their face look like? Make as clear a picture as possible in your mind. Now imagine what this person would look like if they were nervous. What about if they were sad? How would they look confident?

When you are ready, see if you can draw or write about the things that happen when we use our bodies to talk.

12. More feelings – Storyteller notes

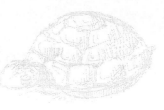

The interaction between mind and body has been studied extensively and we know that the mind and the body are in constant communication with each other as different 'systems' of the body respond to messages from the mind and vice versa. The imagination has an important part to play in this process.

For example, worrying about (or getting excited about) an event long before it happens or even after it has already happened, can cause the body to react as though the event were actually happening now.

It is important for children to have some understanding of how physical feelings and thoughts and emotions are linked. You could explain this in terms of eating healthy food and 'junk' food. For example, when we think thoughts like 'I'm hopeless', 'I can't do this' or 'no one will speak to me', this is like eating 'junk food' – these thoughts affect our body in a negative way. When we have thoughts like, 'I can learn how to do this' or 'this might be difficult but I'm going to have a go', 'it doesn't matter if I make a mistake so long as I try my best', 'I know how to be a good friend', then this is like eating healthy food and these thoughts are good for us.

12. More feelings

Have you ever worried about something that hasn't happened yet? What did your body feel like? Tick the feelings that you get when you are worried.

☐ Butterflies in my tummy   ☐ Heart beats faster

☐ Headache   ☐ Fidget a lot

☐ Feel sick   ☐ Can't think clearly

☐ Tight muscles   ☐ Wobbly knees

Have you ever got *excited* about something long before it happened? What did your body feel like then?

Your imagination can make your body feel different things.

Sometimes this is good but sometimes this is not useful for you.

Sometimes you can change what you are imagining so that you can *feel* better.

13. Feeling tense
– Storyteller notes

Body awareness is an important factor in helping children to understand their emotions. By being aware of how they are physically experiencing their emotions they will also be more aware that they have some choice about controlling these feelings.

Activities 13 and 14 should be done together so that children can feel the difference between being tense and being relaxed. Relate this to Activity sheet 12 as well and re-enforce the idea that we can sometimes change the way that we feel physically in order to have an effect on how we feel emotionally.

13. Feeling tense

When the old man was sad he became cross with himself and the little tortoise thought that he sounded angry. Sometimes we can be feeling one thing but act as though we are feeling something completely different. Sometimes our feelings get all mixed up. So let's think about what our bodies feel like when we have different emotions.

Think of a time when you felt cross about something. I bet your body felt very stiff and perhaps you felt a bit churned up inside? This is called tension. If tension was an animal or a plant or anything else, what would it be? Close your eyes and imagine something that somehow shows us what it's like to be tense.

Imagine that you can become your image of tension. Step into being this plant or animal or object. What does it feel like to be this image?

What does your body feel like? Feel a frown growing from deep inside you. Feel it spreading all the way through you. Really notice what this is like. What is the worst thing about being this image?

Now step out of being this image and back to being you. Give yourself a shake all over… shake your hands, shake your arms, shake your body, shake your legs! Let all that tension disappear.

Draw or write about your image of tension on a sheet of paper.

14. Feeling relaxed
– Storyteller notes

Learning to relax the mind and body is a skill that needs to be practised regularly in order to reap its long-term benefits. Even the most tense-looking children can eventually learn to let go of unnecessary muscle tension during relaxation sessions. Mostly I use a method of focusing on different parts of the body and letting relaxation happen at its own pace. Sometimes I use music to facilitate this. You may have your own favourite method of relaxation. It is worth experimenting with different types over a few sessions and asking for feedback from the children as to which one they found most helpful.

Encourage the children to talk about their pictures of tension and relaxation. Point out some similarities and differences between different children's pictures and also between individual children's images.

14. Feeling relaxed

When we are not tense our body feels more relaxed. If the feeling of relaxing was an animal, a plant or an object, what would it be? Close your eyes and imagine something that somehow shows us what it's like to be relaxed.

Imagine that you can become your image of relaxation. Step into being this plant or animal or object. What does it feel like to be this image?

Feel a smile growing from deep inside you. Feel it spreading all the way through you. Really notice what this is like.

When you are ready, step out of your image again and back to being you. Open your eyes and have a stretch and a yawn!

Draw or write about your feeling of being relaxed.

15. More than one
– Storyteller notes

Talk about the things that we can do to help groups to work well. Invite suggestions as to how different people might feel in a group and how feelings can change from the start of a group to the end of a group. Introduce the idea of endings – that if a particular group/friendship comes to an end that means that something new will be starting. Talk about the feelings that might be associated with this.

15. More than one

The little tortoise wanted to be liked and he wondered if he should try to change in order to 'fit in'. Let's think about what it's like to be part of a group.

What do you think makes a group work well?

Sometimes we may try to 'fit in' with a group because we think we ought to or because it's 'cool' or it's exciting. There may be times when this is OK and also times when it's not OK, when trying to fit in makes us feel awkward or unhappy. What groups do you like to be a part of? Are there any groups that you don't like being in?

16. What makes a good friend?
– Storyteller notes

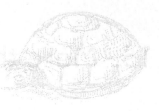

The aim here is to help children to think about what they can do to form friendships, as well as to identify why it is that they 'get on with' a particular friend.

Discuss differences and similarities in people's ideas for their special day. Is there anything that could actually be incorporated into self-esteem sessions?

Discuss the variety of answers that come up and lead this on to a discussion about having friends who are different from each other, i.e. two very different people might be friends with a third person but not particularly close friends with each other. Encourage the children to think why that might be.

16. What makes a good friend?

Saffron and her puppies made friends with the little tortoise and helped him on his journey. Let's think about what makes a good friend. First write down all the words about friendships that you can think of. Make sure you write some feeling words as well as some describing words:

Imagine that it's your 'special friendship day'. Everyone is going to be extra friendly today. They want to know what you like friends to do so that they can be sure to get it right. What will you tell them?

I like it when my friends…

Imagine that it is the end of your special friendship day and you have had a wonderful time with everyone being extra specially friendly. What did you do together? What did you do that helped the day to go well? What were you like with your friends (for example, were you relaxed? Smiley?) How did you feel? What do you feel now? Close your eyes and just imagine…

When you are ready get a sheet of pater and draw or write about your special day.

17. Praise – Storyteller notes

As youngsters we rely heavily on praise and approval to help us to build self-esteem and a strong sense of who we are. It is not long, however, before we have to learn to internalise our praise. In other words, recognise our own achievements and praise ourselves. It is therefore important that we give children a good model to follow by making our praise as descriptive as possible. For example 'well done' has much less of an impact than 'I can see that you have put a lot of thought into your picture. You have used some really interesting shapes and colours', or 'Your picture really shows me what it must feel like when you are tense'.

The word 'good' should also be used with care since it carries a weighty opposite in some children's minds – if I am not 'good' then I am probably 'bad'. The reason for the 'good' should be explained whenever possible. 'Good boy' on its own is not really specific enough (I'm being good but I'm not sure exactly what I've done). 'That's a good piece of work' is also non-specific and potentially judgemental – what then is a 'bad' piece of work? Am I at risk of being bad or doing a bad piece of work without realising it? This is particularly relevant of course when a child has created something – remarks such as 'that's a good picture' or 'that's a good poem', without any explanation of why you think this, might be considered personal opinions rather than descriptions.

17. Praise

The little tortoise felt proud of his decision to leave the store and look for his name. Feeling OK about who you are is really important. There are lots of things that happen to us and around us that help us to feel OK about ourselves, but sometimes things happen that are not so nice, and sometimes we end up feeling 'not OK' about ourselves. We might start to think 'I can't do this' or 'I'm no good at this' or 'everyone has more friends than me.'

This is why praise is so important. It is one of the things that can help us to feel better again. When someone has done something well or really tried hard with something they might be praised for it. The good thing about praise is that it can happen at any time and for *lots* of different reasons. We can praise ourselves and we can praise other people.

To praise someone means…

I can praise people by…

When people praise me I feel…

Today I praised someone for…

Some things I would like to be praised for are…

Today I praised myself for…

18. Talking time – Storyteller notes

It is important for children to understand that not only is it easier for us to talk about important things at certain times, but also that it is easier for others to *listen* at certain times. This helps them to see that sometimes people may not be able to listen fully because of circumstances, rather than because of dislike or rejection of the child or what he has to say.

Examples of easy and difficult times might be:

It's easy when…	*It's harder when…*
• Mum and I are having tea together	• we are rushing to get to school
• I'm happy/relaxed	• I'm angry/tired/ upset/very excited
• I'm with my best friend	• Dad is watching TV
• the other person is listening well	• everyone is talking at the same time
• I'm in a small group	• I'm in a big group
• I know everyone.	• I don't know everyone.

18. Talking time

The little tortoise thought that it was not easy to talk to Saffron and the puppies when they were on their journey to the deserted store. Are there times when you feel that it's difficult for you to say what you want to say? Let's think of some times when it's easy to talk to each other and some times when it's not so easy.

It's easy to talk when...   *It's harder to talk when...*

19. Letting go of worries
– Storyteller notes

Sometimes, if worries can't be talked about or dealt with straight away they do at least need to be deposited somewhere safely. The HugMe tree is designed to be just such a place (but it needs a hug afterwards!). A large paper tree could be put on an appropriate wall, in the classroom or your child's bedroom perhaps, where they can write their worries on paper leaves and hang them up. This idea could also be extended to having a fruit tree – a tree that can have apples or pears or exotic fruit hanging from it, each marked with an achievement, or something that children like about themselves, or perhaps compliments that they could 'pick' to give to someone else.

19. Letting go of worries

The little tortoise had lots of worries to cope with. They made his shell feel heavy. What do you do with your worries? Imagine that there is a huge, strong tree called the HugMe tree. It is so big and has so many branches that it can take all your worries for you.

Draw or write about any worries you might have and hang them on the branches. You can use the HugMe tree at night to hang up your worries before you go to sleep. Just picture it in your mind.

Imagine yourself giving the HugMe tree a great big hug!

20. Any more worries?
– Storyteller notes

Facilitate a discussion about what could happen to the worries. Encourage fantasy solutions as well as more practical ones. For example: they should be tied up in a bundle and sent to _____ who would read each one and discuss them with _____. Laws would be passed to make _____ illegal. Everyone who had ever worried about _____ would receive _____. All the worries would then be _____.

Make a brightly coloured 'worry box' for your home, classroom or clinic room and invite children to post any worries that they may have. Set aside a particular time, perhaps once a week, to check the worry box with the children and 'problem-solve' any worries that are there. Because these will be read out it is, of course, important to tell children who are working in a group that the worries will be brainstormed by everyone (they can be posted anonymously). I know that some schools already use this idea and one of the things to be aware of here is that teachers or therapists may find some worries posted that would need to be taken further because they potentially involve others. Once a worry has been resolved, or the child feels that they are coping with it, then the piece of paper can be ceremoniously torn up or put through the shredder.

20. Any more worries?

Imagine that you could post your worries into a worry box.

What do you think should happen to them then? Where would they go? Would anyone look at them? If so, who would it be? What would they do with them? Draw or write about what happens.

21. The worry team
– Storyteller notes

Ask questions such as 'what would you like to do with your worries? Imagine this happening. What happens next? Then what happens?'

For example, worries can disappear, grow bigger, shrink or change into something else. We could make friends with them, throw them away, send them to the moon, or take them to 'obedience' classes!

Talk about different types of worry. Is there such a thing as a 'useful' worry? What would life be like if we never had any worries?

21. The worry team

Imagine that you are part of a worry team. This is a group of exceptionally clever people who spend their time inventing ways of getting rid of worries. They thought of the HugMe tree and the worry box. Make a list of other things that you could do with worries. How inventive can you be?

22. When being a friend is difficult – Storyteller notes

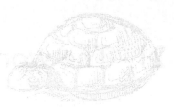

This could be an appropriate point to talk about 'false friends' as well as talk about times when we have difficulties with good friends. Talk about making decisions about friendships based on facts *and* feelings. Talk about the idea of 'working things out' in friendships. Help the children to think specifically about the role they can play in working out disagreements.

(In the story, Spanner turns out not to be a false friend at all, although this is not revealed until later!)

22. When being a friend is difficult

The little tortoise was not sure if Malakaw and Spanner were both false friends. What do you think?

Let's say you and one of your friends disagree about something. Imagine that your friend has come to your house for tea. Your friend wants to play outside and you want to play indoors with a new game that someone has given to you. How does that feel? What might happen?

Imagine that it is time for your friend to go home now and you didn't manage to sort out the disagreement. How do you feel? What happened? What did you do? What didn't you do?

Now imagine that your friend is going home and you did manage to sort things out. You both feel OK. What happened? What did you do? What did you say?

23. Solving problems
– Storyteller notes

Problems are different to worries (see Activity sheets 20–22). Problems are tasks, dilemmas and puzzles that need to be solved.

Brainstorm what to do for some common problems, e.g. you forget to take your lunch to school, your pet hamster gets out of its cage, you accidentally break something in school, someone borrows your pencils and keeps forgetting to give them back.

Sometimes simply naming a problem and taking a good look at it can make it seem a lot less of a problem at all.

It is important to spend some time identifying what steps could *actually* be taken in order to begin to solve the problem.

Encourage recognition of previous experiences of problem solving. It is helpful if children can realise that each time they solve a problem, they are creating new possibilities for themselves.

23. Solving problems

Pepper and the little tortoise both had some problems to solve. As you learn new things, you get better and better at solving problems. For example, maybe you wouldn't know how to untangle a knot in your shoelaces unless you knew how to tie a knot in the first place.

Problems to be solved come in all shapes and sizes. Sometimes we have little problems to solve, like untying knots, and sometimes we have bigger problems, like what to do if our best friend doesn't want to play with us.

Sometimes we have problems that just seem too huge for us to solve on our own.

Imagine if problems were animals or plants or anything at all that could be drawn. What would they be? Fill up a sheet of paper with drawings that somehow show us what little problems and medium-sized problems and really big problems are like.

Choose one of your pictures and give it a name. For example 'friend problem' or 'homework problem'.

Now imagine what you could do to change this first image so that it was easier to deal with.

Draw your problem picture again, adding the changes that you want to make.

How can you help this change to happen in real life? What is the first small thing that you could do that would help?

If I want to solve this problem I could…

24. Still puzzled? – Storyteller notes

Some children are reluctant or even afraid to ask for help when they need it. They may feel that this is further evidence that they are failing and may therefore use other strategies such as watching other children and following their lead or perhaps waiting passively until someone *offers* help. Feeling that it is OK to ask someone to repeat an instruction or that it is OK to say 'I don't understand' is a big step for many children with low self-esteem. Brainstorming this in a very 'matter of fact' way can help them to feel that it is a natural part of the learning process rather than a failure.

Possible strategies might include:

- asking someone to explain it to me

- brainstorming it with other people in the group

- breaking the instruction down into smaller bits and do one bit at a time

- asking for a repetition of the instruction/question.

24. Still puzzled?

Pepper had to think of another way to help the little tortoise when he couldn't carry out his first plan. He had been learning how to solve problems at his patrol lessons and this helped him. Sometimes we all come across problems that we don't understand or that we need help with.

Think about what you need to do if you come across something that you don't understand.

If I don't understand something I could...

25. Moving – Storyteller notes

Physical achievements are an important element in building and maintaining self-esteem for many children. A physical achievement might be something like climbing a tree, swimming two lengths of the pool, standing on one leg for one minute, running very fast. Children with restricted movement potential will also have important experiences of mastering physical skills which they can share with others.

25. Moving

The little tortoise learned how to move a little bit by rocking from side to side. He felt good about this; it was a big achievement for him. He enjoyed the feeling of moving on wheels as well.

If you could win an award for an achievement that involved something physical what would you like the award to be for?

Why does physical exercise and physical achievement help us to feel good?

26. Confidence – Storyteller notes

Confidence is quite a hard concept to grasp and yet most children with low self-esteem have the idea that they somehow need more of it. One way of exploring what confidence is all about is to think of someone that the children all agree *appears* confident. This might be a TV personality or a fictional character or someone they all know. Make a list together of all the things that seem to make them appear confident. Be as specific as possible. For example, if someone says 'they *look* confident', then talk about how the person stands, walks, sits, dresses, etc. If they say 'they *sound* confident', talk about *how* they sound – Fast? Slow? Loud? Quiet? Somewhere in-between?

26. Confidence

During his journey, the little tortoise built up a lot of confidence. What does the word 'confidence' mean?

Some people can seem to be very confident. Most of us are confident in some of the things we do and in some places. We have to build up our confidence with other things.

   Think about one thing that you would like to be able to do with more confidence.

   I would like to be more confident when…

Now think of a time when you have felt confident in the past. Draw or write about it here.

   A time when I felt confident was…

Table of Expansion Topics Relevant to the English National Curriculum Guidelines for PSHE and Citizenship (Key Stage 1)

Reference	'Pupils should be taught...'	Chapter	Expansion topics	Activity sheets
KS1 1b	To share their opinions on things that matter to them and explain their views	All	• Encourage discussion about each stage of the story. What does the tortoise learn in each chapter?	
KS1 1c	To recognise, name and deal with their feelings in a positive way	1	• Collect feeling words and talk about different times that people might feel different emotions.	1, 2
		1	• How do you think the old man was feeling?	
		2	• Talk about how feelings can change from one moment to the next. What sorts of things help you to feel happy?	9, 10
		2	• How do we show that we are feeling anxious? How do we show that we are feeling angry or happy?	11
		3	• Talk about how when someone is sad they can sometimes sound or act as though they are angry. Talk about how we can sometimes mix up our feelings. Talk about the effects of different emotions on the body.	12–14
		5	• Talk about talking. Whom can you talk to about things that worry you?	
		5	• Talk about what can be done with worries.	
		6	• How do you think the little tortoise and Pepper were feeling? Do you think they were feeling the same feelings as each other or different feelings? Why do you think they were feeling these things? Did they have a choice about how they were feeling?	19–21

Reference	'Pupils should be taught…'	Chapter	Expansion topics	Activity sheets
KS1 1d	To think about themselves, learn from their experiences and recognise what they are good at	1	• Has anyone ever called you by the wrong name? What would you feel if someone made a mistake about who you are or what you have done/haven't done? When would that be OK? When would it not be OK?	
		1	• If you were an animal, what animal would you be? What would you call yourself? Why?	
		2	• Have you ever thought about what it would be like to be someone else? First think about what it is like to be you. Then think what it would be like to be someone else for a day.	7–8
		4	• Talk about feeling good about being you. Talk about praise.	
		5	• Talk about making mistakes and trying again. How is this useful?	
		6	• How do you solve problems?	
		6	• Talk about why physical achievements help us to feel good about ourselves.	23, 24, 25
		7	• Talk about coping with unexpected things.	
		7	• Talk about times when you felt brave enough or confident enough to do something that was a bit difficult for you.	26
KS1 2a	To take part in discussions with one other person and the whole class	All	• There are opportunities for this throughout the story.	

Continued on next page

Reference	'Pupils should be taught…'	Chapter	Expansion topics	Activity sheets
	To recognise choices they can make, and recognise the difference between right and wrong	3	• How do you make decisions? What helps you to make a decision?	
		3	• Use a 'tunnel of thoughts' to explore the little tortoise's dilemma. Should he stay or should he leave the store?	
KS1 2c		6	• Think of a time when you have made a choice about what to do or where to go and you felt that you made the right choice. How many different situations can you think of where you have a choice about things? Are there any situations you can think of when you don't have a choice?	
KS1 2d	To agree and follow rules for their group and classroom, and understand how rules help them	5	• Make a group/class list of times when it's easy to talk to people and times when it's harder to talk to people. Agree on strategies to use when what you have to say is important. Agree on strategies/rules for talking during a story session. See also KS1 4b.	18
KS1 2f	That they belong to various groups and communities, such as family and school	3	• Use 'thought bubbling' to talk about trying to 'fit in' with a group. What does the tortoise feel about staying in the store?	15
		4	• Talk about what makes a good friend.	
		5	• Talk about when being friends with someone is difficult. Talk about 'false' friends.	
		7	• Talk about different perspectives.	
KS1 4a	To recognise how their behaviour affects other people	7	• Talk about how the 'stories' of each of our lives join with or touch the stories of other people's lives too.	

Reference	'Pupils should be taught…'	Chapter	Expansion topics	Activity sheets
KS1 4b	To listen to other people and play and work co-operatively	5	• Make a group/class list of times when it's easy to talk to people and times when it's harder to talk to people. Agree on strategies to use when what you have to say is important. Agree on strategies/rules for classroom talking.	18
KS1 4c	To identify and respect the differences and similarities between people	1	• Where is Mauritius? What would it be like to live in a different country? What would you like/not like about being in a different place? What sort of things do you think would be the same/different?	
		2	• Talk about 'what if everyone in the world was exactly the same. What might be good about this? What might not be so good? What is good about having things in common with others?	5, 6
KS1 4d	That family and friends should care for each other	3	• Talk about asking for/accepting help from teachers, friends and family.	
		5	• How do you think the tortoise felt when Saffron and the pups had to go away to do other things?	
KS1 4e	That there are different types of teasing and bullying, that bullying is wrong, and how to get help to deal with bullying	1	• Is there a difference between teasing and bullying? What does it feel like to be teased or bullied? How can you deal with teasing?	3, 4

Source: QCA National Curriculum online. © QCA.

Explanation of Drama Strategies

For further ideas see Primary National Strategy leaflets produced by the Department for Education and Skills (DfES Publications).

> ### Note
> These drama techniques are widely used in schools but are similar to some strategies used in *drama therapy*. The following outlines are *not* descriptions of therapy strategies. However, even at this level of use, it is extremely important to make sure that the children have stepped out of role after completion of the activity. The release of role should be physical, emotional and mental and this can be done by simple means such as asking the children to name and put away any props they have used and by getting them to shake their arms and hands and shout their own name.

Hot-seating

This encourages children to explore the skill of empathising with another person's point of view or feelings.

A member of the group sits in the 'hot seat' in role as one of the characters from the story. The rest of the group are invited to ask this person questions in order to explore perceived feelings and situations from the character's perspective. Questions can be spontaneous or briefly planned beforehand.

Tunnel of thoughts

(Also known as conscience alley or decision alley)
The group form two lines facing each other. One person takes on the role of a character in the story who is faced with a decision or dilemma. This character walks down the centre of the tunnel as the rest of the group speak out thoughts in support of both sides of the decision (e.g. I should stay

because_____, I should leave because _____). The character, having consulted his 'conscience' in this way, has choice about what thoughts to take on board and what to discard. He then makes his decision on reaching the end of the tunnel.

Thought bubbling

(Also known as thought tracking)
This is a way of exploring the 'private' thoughts of a character, usually at a point of crisis or dilemma in a story. One person takes on the role of the character and the rest of the group stand in a circle around her and take turns to 'speak the thought' that the character might be having at that particular point in the narrative. These thoughts might be different to or the same as the thoughts that the character is actually speaking.

This can also be done in pairs, where two people take on the same character role and speak two different perspectives while the rest of the group ask questions about their actions and choices.

Paired improvisation

Two people take on the roles of two different characters and have a conversation for a pre-set period of time and with no prior planning.

Pictures to Colour In

The little tin tortoise

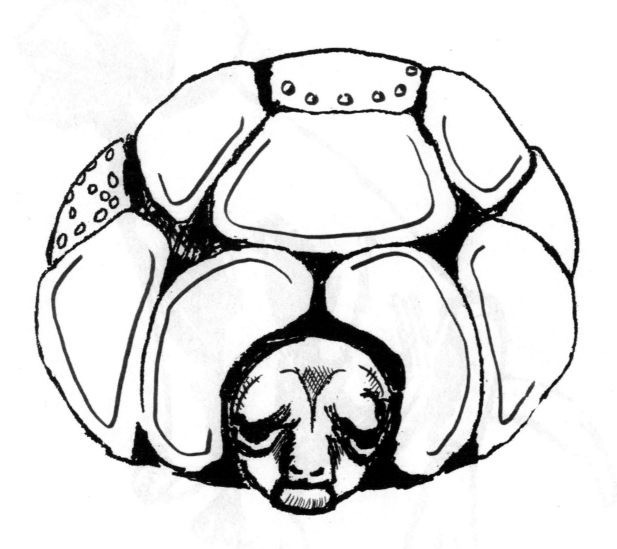

The little tin tortoise

Coco

Malakaw

Lovena

Spanner